TATTERED SECRETS

THE BILLIONAIRES OF CREST STRATEGIES
BOOK 2

ELORA RAE

ALSO BY ELORA RAE

The Billionaires Of Crest Strategies

Ruined Lies

Tattered Secrets

Salvaged Vows

Coded Truths

Wrecked Fates

To everyone who wants to be protected, worshipped, and slightly stalked.

TRIGGER/CONTENT WARNING

Hey gorgeous (likely unhinged) readers!

This novella is a dark billionaire romance.

Before you dive into Benedict and Paisley's deliciously complicated love story, let's chat about what you're getting into because we all know that in this genre, content warnings are how we choose books...

Inside this book, you'll find:
- **Long-term surveillance and obsession:** Benedict has been watching the Paisley for twelve years, tracking her movements and her life
- **Violence and blood:** Including kidnapping, shootings, and slight gore
- **Excessive swearing and profanity:** These characters have filthy mouths in more ways than one
- **Spicy, high-heat sex scenes:** Including oral sex, rough consensual sex, and anal

Other content warnings: Mild choking during sex, sex in semi-public places, discussion of suicide, murder (including discussion of murder-suicide plans), gun violence, characters being shot, physical assault between friends, betrayal of trust, and professional/personal boundaries being repeatedly crossed.

I did say it was dark...

The good news? This is a consensual romance with clear boundaries between our main characters. The darkness comes from external threats and morally gray professional choices, not from toxic relationship dynamics.

If any of these themes are upsetting or not your thing, please take care while reading, or maybe skip this one. There are lots of amazing books out there, so find the ones that bring you joy, not stress.

But if you're here for a tense, sexy, high-stakes story where you'll root for the handsome billionaire who has been pining after his best friend's little sister for twelve years...

Welcome to the *Billionaires of Crest Strategies*.

You've been warned.

Happy reading!

-Elora

CHAPTER ONE

BENEDIT

No amount of money could buy the heart of Paisley Crest, and that knowledge killed Benedict Astor as he watched his best friend's sister steal the hearts of every man and woman in the ballroom.

Benedict positioned himself where he always did. In the shadows, where he could see everything without being seen. The dim corner of the ballroom afforded him the perfect vantage point to observe the charity gala's attendees, but his gaze tracked only one person.

Paisley Crest.

She moved through the crowd in a deep blue silk dress that clung to curves he'd memorized from years of watching from afar. The fabric caught the light when she turned, creating shadows and highlights across her body that he could have mapped with his eyes closed. She'd pinned up her dark curls, exposing the nape. He would've paid anything to press his lips there. To feel her soft skin. Hear her moan against him.

This was his purgatory. Watching. Wanting. Never having.

God, Carson would kill Benedict if he knew that his best friend and business partner was in love with his baby sister.

Benedict adjusted his collar. It was too hot in there. It certainly had nothing to do with the effect Paisley had on him. The damn tie was just too tight. And his trousers. They were feeling too tight too when just a little while ago, before a certain distraction arrived, his suit had been impeccable, his posture perfect, his expression neutral. Only his gaze revealed the truth as it followed her.

He was her protector. At least, that's what he told himself to justify the way he kept track of her.

"You look like you're planning a hit," Carson said, appearing at Benedict's side with two whiskeys. He handed one to Benedict. "Stop scowling. It's a party."

Benedict accepted the drink without shifting his gaze. "I don't have to be the face of the company. That's your job." He poked Carson in the chest.

"So you're saying I can't pay you to switch places with me?" Carson teased.

"There is not enough money in the world. Besides," Benedict took a slow sip of whiskey, letting it burn down his throat. "I have every-thing I want."

Except Paisley.

Carson snorted. "I suppose that's true." He clapped Benedict's shoulder. "I guess I should go mingle. I'll send you a text if I need rescuing."

"I'll make sure to put my phone on do not disturb."

Benedict smirked, watching as Carson flipped him off and rejoined the party. His best friend commanded attention in a way Benedict never could. Carson's easy confidence was why he was the face of their reputation management business. Not Benedict, and certainly not the other three men, though James would do well. Better than Tanner or Penn.

Across the room, Paisley laughed at something someone said, the sound carrying over the ambient noise. Benedict tensed, finding her instantly.

He took another sip of whiskey, watching as a man approached her, leaning in too close. Bastard. Benedict's fingers tightened around the glass, knuckles whitening. The stranger's hand settled on the small of her back, and Benedict's jaw clenched hard enough to hurt.

Twelve years. He'd been in this private hell for twelve years.

He'd met her at Carson's birthday celebration. Benedict had been twenty-one himself, fresh out of college and working his way through business school, determined to build something that would matter.

Carson had made the introduction. Paisley had been a beautiful young woman of eighteen with wild curls and freckles scattered across her nose. She'd worn a simple sundress, nothing fancy. And yet Benedict had choked on his drink at the sight of her.

When he'd introduced himself, extending his hand, she'd ignored it, instead throwing her arms around him and telling him that any friend of Carson's was family to her.

The hug had lasted seconds. Maybe less. But in that moment, with her pressed against him and the scent of her shampoo filling his lungs, Benedict had known with absolute certainty that Paisley Crest would ruin him.

That certainty had only grown stronger over the years.

Benedict watched as Paisley extricated herself from the man's grasp with a smile. She had a gift for letting people down without making them feel rejected. It was part of what made her so dangerous to him. She held genuine kindness in those brown eyes, and she actually cared about everyone's feelings.

Everyone except his, because she had no idea how he felt.

His phone vibrated in his pocket. A text from a person who worked under him.

> Surveillance is complete for the Hamilton case.
> Files uploaded to secure server.

Benedict replied with a simple acknowledgment. Crest Strategies never stopped working, even during their own charity events. Carson might be the face, but Benedict was the spine, the one who kept everything aligned, who anticipated problems before they materialized.

Which was why he noticed immediately when Paisley's behavior shifted.

She'd been in the middle of a conversation with the nonprofit director when her phone lit up. Her expression changed. Though she still smiled, her eyes tightened and her lips parted. Excusing herself, she turned and moved toward the exit.

Benedict set his glass down. Something was wrong.

He tracked her movement through the crowd, maintaining his distance but never losing sight of her. She slipped through the ballroom doors, bypassing the coat check and heading for the private elevator—the one that led to the Crest Strategies offices upstairs.

Benedict waited thirty seconds before following. The elevator was already gone when he reached it, the digital display showing it had stopped at the office suite.

He pressed the call button, keeping his face neutral despite the confusion churning inside him. Why would Paisley go to their offices during the gala? The entire staff was downstairs. The offices would be empty.

When the elevator arrived, he stepped inside and pressed the button, then leaned against the wall as the doors closed. His mind cataloged possibilities: perhaps she needed something from Carson's office? Maybe she'd forgotten an item earlier in the day when she'd stopped by to have lunch with her brother?

None of the explanations felt right.

The elevator doors opened onto the darkened reception area. The motion sensors detected his presence, illuminating the space with soft light. Benedict moved through the familiar halls, listening for any sound that might reveal Paisley's location.

The main workspace was empty. So was the conference room. He moved down the hallway toward the executive offices, pausing outside each door to listen before continuing.

When he reached Carson's office at the end of the hall, the sound of pages moving slipped through the crack in the door inside. It was ajar, a sliver of light spilling into the corridor. Benedict approached, moving as quietly as he could, and he positioned himself to see through the narrow opening without being seen.

Paisley stood at Carson's desk, rifling through papers. She chewed on the edge of her thumb as she scanned the lines of text. Her brow furrowed. She flipped to the next. And the next.

She was searching for something specific.

Benedict watched as she opened a drawer, removed a file, and began photographing its contents with her phone. His blood ran cold. This wasn't innocent. This was... infiltration.

He pushed the door open. "Pai?"

She jumped, dropping her phone with a clatter. When she turned to face him, her eyes were wide. A second later, though, a strained grin replaced the surprise.

"Ben." His name came out breathless. She pressed a hand to her chest. "You scared me."

"What are you doing in here?" He kept his voice even.

"I just needed to grab something from Carson's office." A lie. She'd lied to his face. Benedict had studied her expressions, cataloged her tells. The slight flutter of her eyelashes. The way she chewed the inside of her cheek or the edge of her thumb.

"Try again." He stepped into the office, closing the door behind him. "This time with the truth."

Paisley's shoulders slumped. She bent to retrieve her phone, tucking it into her clutch. "It's not what it looks like."

"It looks like you're going through your brother's confidential files and photographing them." Benedict moved closer, his footsteps silent on the plush carpet. "Please tell me there's an explanation that doesn't involve corporate espionage."

"Corporate espionage?" She laughed, but it sounded hollow. "Don't be dramatic."

"Then what is it?" He was close enough now to smell her perfume; something floral with undertones of vanilla. Close enough to see the pulse jumping in her throat.

"I can't tell you." She met his gaze, chin lifted in defiance. "But I need you to trust me."

"Trust works both ways." He gestured to the open file on the desk. "This doesn't look like trust."

She took a step toward him, and Benedict battled the urge to retreat. It didn't matter that she barely came up to his chest. Paisley Crest could be just as intimidating as her brother when she wanted to be. It also didn't help that being this close to her was dangerous. She made it harder to think, to remember why he needed to keep his distance.

"There are things about Crest Strategies that you don't know," she whispered. "Things Carson is hiding."

Benedict's expression remained impassive, but his mind raced. "Your brother and I built this company together. There's nothing about it I don't know."

"Are you sure about that?" Her gaze searched his face. "The Jennings account. Have you looked into it personally?"

"I know what it is."

"It's a high-profile divorce case you all took about five months ago."

"I'm aware." He shrugged, sliding his hands into his pockets. "I was in charge of the surveillance. But why do you care about it?"

"The wife." Paisley's voice dropped to a whisper. "She disappeared two days ago."

"People disappear all the time during contentious divorces." His response was automatic. "They go to friends, family, hotels under assumed names."

"Police found her car abandoned on the side of the road. Blood in the trunk."

A chill ran down Benedict's spine. "And you think this has some-thing to do with us? Really? Come on, Pai." He frowned at her. "We're the good guys here."

Well, most of the time.

There had been occasions where Crest Strategies had used its resources to put well-deserving criminals into the metaphorical ground. But he knew for a fact that the Jennings case was not one of them. The wife had been their client. Their job was to protect her and help her win her case against her abusive husband.

Benedict was about to point this out when Paisley continued.

"I think it has something to do with Tanner." Paisley held up her phone, showing him a series of text messages. "He's been in contact with Jenning's private security team. Secret meetings, off the books."

Benedict's mind processed the information, even as he shook his head. If what she was saying was true, it meant someone at Crest Strategies—someone he trusted—was operating outside their ethical boundaries. Outside the law. Sure, Tanner was the go-to clean-up guy, but they reserved that for messier cases. Mrs. Jennings was an easy client.

"Tanner wouldn't do that." Benedict straightened, rolling his shoulders back. At least, he thought, not without Carson's instructions.

"Why are you investigating this?" he asked. "Why not go to the police?"

"With what evidence? Text messages that could be about anything?" She shook her head. "I needed proof before I brought this to Carson. Or to you."

"You think I'm involved." It wasn't a question.

"I think you see the best in your friends." Her expression softened. "Even when evidence suggests otherwise."

"You just said you don't have evidence."

"Well, that's what I was looking for." She gestured towards the desk.

Benedict closed his eyes, forcing himself to think logically rather than emotionally. He doubted reserved and controlled Tanner had gone rogue. For Tanner to make things or people disappear, all five Crest Strategies men had to agree, and they hadn't even discussed it. But if Paisley was right, though he still doubted she was, and his friend was involved in something illegal, they needed to handle it themselves before it destroyed everything they'd built.

"Alright," he said, sighing. "Show me what you've found." He moved to the desk, standing close enough that their shoulders almost touched.

Paisley hesitated, then pulled out her phone again. "These are texts between Tanner and Mr. Jennings from last week." She scrolled through screenshots. "And these are surveillance photos my contact took of them meeting at a warehouse in the industrial district."

Benedict studied the images. "Your contact?" His mind calculated potential damage and containment strategies. "Who else knows about this?"

"Just me." She bit the side of her thumbnail.

"And this contact." He shook his head. "Who is it, Pai? Who sent you these?"

"I...I can't tell you." She put her phone away and took a step back. "Sorry, but I couldn't risk going to Carson until I was certain. He and Tanner are too close."

"And you thought I'd be more objective?" He raised an eyebrow.

"Well, you didn't give me much of a choice, barreling in here." She dropped his gaze. "But I did think you'd be more rational." Her eyes met his. "You almost always are."

The compliment shouldn't have affected him, but it did. Even now, with everything she'd implied about his friend, a treacherous warmth spread through his chest.

"What are you going to do now that you know?" She asked as she wrapped her arms around herself. "Are you going to tell Carson about all of this?"

"I..." Benedict ran a hand through his sandy blonde hair and shook his head. "I don't know."

His mind raced through calculations and consequences. The possibility that Tanner was operating outside their established protocols felt like a crack in the foundation of everything he'd built with Carson. It also was unlikely. But there was something else clouding his judgment. Or rather, someone. The woman standing before him, her brown eyes wide with concern, waiting for his answer.

"I really should tell Carson," he said, rubbing the back of his neck. "But..."

"But what?" Paisley stepped closer, her perfume invading his senses again.

"But I need to verify your information first." His voice remained steady despite the chaos in his mind. "If I go to Carson with accusations against Tanner without concrete evidence, it could fracture everything."

"So you'll help me?" Hope brightened her expression.

Benedict closed his eyes. This was dangerous territory. Getting involved in Paisley's investigation meant spending time with her. Alone. It meant trusting her judgment. It meant keeping secrets from Carson.

It meant being near her. Constantly.

Maybe that's what pushed him over the edge.

"Yes," he finally said, opening his eyes to find her watching him with her beautiful wide eyes. "I'll help you. But we do this my way. That means no more sneaking around, especially in Carson's office. This room is off limits when he's not here, even for me. God only knows what he'd do if he found out we were in here."

Relief softened her features. "Thank you, Benny."

The nickname sent an electric current through him that gathered at the base of his spine.

"Don't thank me yet." He moved to Carson's desk, carefully returning the files to their original positions. "This could be nothing. Or it could be something that destroys Crest Strategies. And then we're all screwed."

"Or saves it," she countered, helping him reorganize the desk.

Their hands brushed as they both reached for the same folder. Benedict froze, shocks shooting up his arm from that simple contact. Paisley paused too, her gaze darting to his face before glancing away.

"Sorry," she murmured, withdrawing her hand.

Benedict cleared his throat. "We should get back to the event before someone notices we're both missing."

"Right." She nodded, but made no move to leave. Instead, she chewed her bottom lip. "Ben, there's something else, but I need you to promise not to freak out."

"Freak out?" He turned to face her. "Why would I freak out?"

"It's just...I've felt for a while that someone's been... watching me." Her voice dropped to just above a whisper. "Following me, maybe. I thought I was being paranoid, but I noticed the same car

9

outside my building and my office, and... I don't know. It feels off. And I thought maybe, with you being in charge of surveillance and all, you might be willing to look into it."

Benedict froze. He'd been monitoring her for years, for her protection, he told himself, but he'd been meticulous, invisible. If she'd sensed surveillance, it wasn't his.

Which meant someone else was watching Paisley.

"When did this start?" His voice came out sharper than intended.

"A few months ago. Just... feelings at first. Then I noticed the car multiple nights in a row."

Benedict's protective instincts surged forward, drowning out his professional detachment. "Description?"

"Dark sedan. Tinted windows. I couldn't see the driver."

His mind was already mapping security protocols, calculating risks. "You should stay at Carson's until we figure this out."

"Hell no." She shook her head. "I'm not running scared. It might be nothing. And I'm not telling Carson until we know what's happening."

Their gazes locked in a silent battle. Benedict recognized the stubborn set of her jaw. It was the same expression Carson wore when he'd made up his mind.

"Fine then, you'll stay with me," he said before he could stop himself.

Paisley's eyes widened. "What?"

"My penthouse has state-of-the-art security. No one gets in without my knowledge. It's the logical solution."

A slow blush crept across her cheeks. "You want me to move in with you?"

"Temporarily," he clarified, ignoring how his heart raced at the thought. "For your protection."

"Carson will be pissed."

"Why? I'd like to think he'd appreciate me looking after his little sister."

Her face dropped, and she gave a small nod. "Right. His little sister." The small chuckle she gave lacked any heart. "I suppose all five of you see me that way."

He wanted to tell her he didn't. Instead, he bit his tongue hard enough to draw blood.

"Okay," she said. "When do I move in?"

"Tonight." His voice dropped lower. "After the event."

"Tonight then," she repeated.

CHAPTER TWO

PAISLEY

PAISLEY STOOD IN THE MIDDLE OF BENEDICT'S PENTHOUSE, clutching her overnight bag to her chest. The surrounding space was nothing like she'd imagined.

And she'd imagined it plenty of times.

"You can put your things in the guest room." Benedict gestured down a hallway. "Second door on the right."

"Thanks." She couldn't meet his eyes. Not now, when they were alone in his private space, the place he returned to each night.

The place he ate.

And showered.

And probably slept with many other women.

God, what she wouldn't give to be one of those women.

Unlike her brother's sterile minimalist apartment with its monochrome palette and uncomfortable furniture designed to discourage lingering, Benedict's home felt... lived in. Bookshelves lined one wall, packed with worn paperbacks and leather-bound classics. A record player sat in the corner beside a collection of vinyl that would make her father jealous. In the center of the living room sat a deep blue sectional and buttery leather armchairs. She wanted to grab a book and sink into one.

It wasn't what she expected from a man who presented such a controlled exterior to the world.

"I'll show you around." Benedict moved past her, close enough that his expensive cedar cologne wafted towards her.

Her brain malfunctioned.

Twelve years. That's how long she'd been in love with him. Twelve years of watching him from across rooms, of making excuses to visit Carson at the office just to catch a glimpse of Benedict's rare smile. Twelve years of him looking through her, of being Carson's little sister and nothing more.

She followed him down the hallway, past framed black and white photographs of cityscapes she didn't recognize. His shoulders filled the space, his crisp white shirt stretching across his back as he walked. She knew about the wolf tattoo beneath that fabric, and had dreamt about tracing it with her fingers on more than one occasion. God bless the Crest Strategies beach days. The memory still visited her on lonely nights.

"Your bathroom's here." He pushed open the door to reveal gleaming marble and glass. "Guest room." Another door. "And my office is at the end of the hall. That's off-limits."

Paisley raised an eyebrow. "Why? Planning world domination in there?"

A ghost of a smile touched his lips. "Something like that. Can't work with Cars forever." He winked at her, then nodded towards the guest room. "I hope it'll be all right for you."

The walls room were painted a soft blue, with a king-sized bed dressed in light grey linens. A desk sat beneath a window with a view of the city skyline.

"Sorry it's not much," he said, leaning against the doorway. "I don't have many overnight guests."

"It's perfect." She set her bag on the bed. "Thank you for doing this. I know it's an imposition."

Benedict's ice-blue gaze studied her face. "It's not."

"What's our exit strategy for when my brother finds out?" she asked, breaking eye contact first. She dug through her purse and pulled out her phone while she spoke. "I'll write your eulogy if you write mine."

Her smile faltered for a moment when she noticed the unread text. Her contact. He'd messaged her asking for the photos.

Definitely not something she needed to be thinking about with the man who could read anyone like a book blocking the doorway.

She smiled, hoping he hadn't noticed her slip. "Think he'll make it quick?"

"You're just staying here. It's not like anything is going to happen between us."

"Right." Paisley pinched her lips together, hiding the grimace that wanted to break free. "That would be totally out of the box."

"Exactly." He shrugged, his gaze dropping to her phone for a second before he looked back at her face. "Besides, until we know what we're dealing with, you're safer here. If someone's watching you and it's connected to the Jennings case—"

"Carson will still lose his mind," she finished.

"Pretty much." Benedict ran a hand through his perfectly styled hair, mussing it slightly. The gesture was so uncharacteristically vulnerable that Paisley's heart stuttered. "Carson's protective of you. We all are."

There it was again. The reminder of how they saw her. A little sister to be protected, not a woman to be desired.

"Well, thanks." She forced a smile. "The Crest Strategies boys' club looking out for poor little Paisley."

Something flickered across his face. "That's not—"

"It's fine." She waved him off. "I appreciate it. Really."

An awkward silence fell between them.

"I'll let you get settled." Benedict stepped back. "Kitchen's stocked if you're hungry. Make yourself at home."

He disappeared down the hallway to his office, leaving Paisley alone with an ache in her heart and the lingering scent of his cologne.

By midnight, they'd established an uneasy rhythm. Benedict worked in his home office with the door cracked, occasionally taking calls in hushed tones. Paisley curled in an armchair with one of his books, but she actually spent most of the time on her phone going over the pictures she'd taken in her brother's office.

She glanced down the hallway toward the sliver of light from Benedict's office, then back at her phone. Marcus's text from earlier glowed on the screen.

> Did you get the files? Need to know what they're hiding before it's too late.

She chewed her thumbnail. A few months ago, she would have laughed if someone had suggested she'd be spying on her own brother. Then Marcus had approached her after one of her nonprofit's fundraisers. He'd seemed concerned and professional even when he'd presented her with evidence that suggested Crest Strategies was burying something terrible. At first, she'd dismissed him, defending her brother as she had her entire life. But then came the photos, the timeline discrepancies, the financial records that didn't add up. What if Carson was protecting Tanner or someone dangerous? What if he'd gotten in too deep? She couldn't stand by if innocent people were being hurt.

Her thumb hovered over the phone. She wasn't betraying Carson. She never would. She loved her older brother, even if he did annoy the shit out of her most weekdays. But Marcus had offered her a chance to save him before things got out of control. Really, she was saving him from himself. If it were true, that is. Benedict's voice echoed in her mind. If there was something sinister happening at Crest Strategies, she needed to find it before the authorities did. Family protected family, even from themselves.

"You should get some sleep."

Paisley jumped, nearly dropping her phone. Benedict stood against the wall, his tie loosened and sleeves rolled up to reveal strong forearms. The casual dishevelment made him look younger, more approachable. More dangerous to her heart.

"I'm not tired," she lied, quickly locking her screen. "Just reading."

Benedict's gaze lingered on her phone before returning to her face. "Practicing your upside-down reading skills?"

Heat rushed to her cheeks as she glanced down at the upside-down novel in her lap. "I was just... thinking."

"About what you found in Carson's office?" He moved into the room, settling into the chair opposite hers. Benedict leaned forward, his elbows on his knees and his hands clasped below his chin.

"Among other things." She set the book aside. "I'm worried about him."

"Carson can take care of himself."

"Are we talking about the same Carson?" She leaned back. "You've known him longer than most. Well, besides me. Haven't you noticed how he's changed since Emma?"

Pain flickered across Benedict's face. "We all changed after Emma."

"But he's gotten colder. More secretive." She twisted her fingers together. "Sometimes I feel like I don't know who my brother is anymore."

"Anyone would change after someone they loved died." Benedict studied her face. "Why were you really in his office tonight?"

Something about Benedict's steady gaze made her want to confess everything. About Marcus and his concerns about Crest Strategies. About her fears for her older brother going down a dark path ever since his fiancee killed herself. About Paisley's own gigantic, ridiculous crush on Benedict.

"I told you. I think something's wrong with the Jennings case."

"Really? Is that the only reason?" His voice remained neutral.

"Yes. No." Her voice dropped to a whisper. "Ben, please. I'm scared for him."

Softness shifted his expression. "Nothing will happen to Carson. He's got too many people looking out for him." He glanced down at the Rolex around his wrist. "It's late. We should go to bed. I've got an early meeting with Penn in the morning about a new surveillance system we'll be implementing soon."

When he stood and offered her a hand, she took it and let him pull her up. They stood face to face for a second before Benedict dropped her hand and stepped back.

"Do you want tea before bed?" He cleared his throat, glancing over his shoulder towards the kitchen.

"That would be nice." She followed him, leaning against the counter as he filled a kettle. "So," she ventured, "how long have you lived here?"

"Five years." He placed two mugs on the counter. "I was further downtown before, but I like how short the commute is from work now."

"It's nice. More..." She searched for the right word. "Homey than I expected."

A smile tugged at his lips. "What did you expect? A villain's lair? Secret surveillance room?"

If only he knew how close to the truth that was. The image she'd constructed of his apartment over the years had definitely included some sort of high-tech command center where he monitored the world.

"Something like Carson's place," she admitted. "All chrome and emptiness."

Benedict's smile widened. "Cars's apartment is a hotel room he happens to own."

Paisley laughed. "God, it really is. Remember when I bought him that houseplant for Christmas?"

"The one that died within a week?"

"He forgot to water it!" She shook her head. "Said it didn't try hard enough to survive.'"

Benedict handed her a steaming mug. Their fingers brushed, and Paisley nearly dropped it.

"Careful," he murmured. "It's hot."

She nodded, not trusting her voice. They stood in companionable silence for a while, staring out at the city skyline beyond his arched windows.

"I should get some sleep," she finally said. "It's been a long day."

Benedict nodded. "Of course. I'll be up for a while if you need anything."

In the guest room, Paisley changed into sleep shorts and an oversized t-shirt, then slid beneath the cool sheets. The sound of Benedict moving around the apartment kept her awake. Water running, a door closing, the soft pad of footsteps.

God, it was going to be a long night.

———

MORNING BROUGHT SUNSHINE STREAMING THROUGH unfamiliar windows and the smell of coffee. Paisley blinked awake, momentarily disoriented before remembering where she was.

Benedict's penthouse. Benedict's guest room. Benedict's sheets against her skin.

She dragged herself out of bed and into the bathroom, wincing at her reflection. Her waves stuck out in every direction, and yesterday's mascara had smudged beneath her eyes. Splashing water on her face, she attempted to make herself presentable before venturing out. Unfortunately, presentable meant no make up and a messy bun because she'd forgotten to pack her essentials in her rush.

Benedict stood at the kitchen island, already dressed in a tailored gray suit, scrolling through his phone. He looked up when she entered, his gaze sweeping over her sleep-rumpled form before quickly returning to his screen.

"Morning," he said, voice carefully neutral. "Coffee's ready."

"Thanks." She padded to the coffeemaker, acutely aware of her bare legs and messy hair. "Are you ready for your meeting?"

"Almost." He set down his phone. "I'll be gone most of the day."

Disappointment curled in her stomach. "Oh."

"Will you be okay here alone?" He looked at her properly now, his gaze lingering on her hair in a way that made her regret not taking a shower at least. "You can work from here. The Wi-Fi password is on the fridge."

"I'll be fine." She poured coffee into a mug that read 'WORLD'S OKAYEST STRATEGIST'—clearly a gag gift, probably from Carson. "I have some work with the nonprofit to catch up on anyway."

Benedict hesitated, then reached into his pocket and produced a key. "In case you need to go out. Though I'd prefer if you stayed in until we know more about who might be watching you."

Their fingers touched as she took the key. This time, she didn't imagine the slight intake of his breath.

"Be careful, Benny," she said.

"Always am."

And then he was gone, leaving Paisley alone in his space, surrounded by pieces of the real Benedict Astor that few people ever saw.

By noon, Paisley had explored every inch of the penthouse except his office. Not that she hadn't been tempted. And tried. But the bastard had locked the door.

She sat at the dining room table, her legs crossed under her, as she typed up an email response to a donor.

When her phone chimed from a text from Marcus, her fingers froze on the keyboard.

> Any update on those files?

Her stomach knotted. She hadn't sent the photos from Carson's office yet, not after Benedict's warning and request to let him look into things. Something about the whole situation felt off.

> Still working on it.

Three dots appeared immediately.

> Time sensitive, Ms. Crest. People could get hurt if we don't act.

She bit down on her thumbnail as she considered a response. There wasn't time though, before her phone chimed again. He'd attached a file.

> Found these. Thought you should see them.

19

She hesitated before opening it. Inside were financial records showing transfers from Crest Strategies accounts to offshore holdings, all bearing Carson's electronic signature. And worse—audio files.

She played the first one with trembling fingers.

"The money needs to be clean by Friday." Carson's voice rang through her phone speaker. "Jennings can't know where it came from."

Another voice responded, and she recognized it as Tanner Whitney's. "Already handled. Penn's setting up the shell companies now."

Paisley's heart pounded. Penn? Involved too?

Another audio file sounded, again with Carson's voice. "If anyone asks questions, we deny everything."

A text from Marcus followed.

> Your brother's involved in money laundering. They all are. We need to expose this before more people get hurt, but I can't do it without your help.

She shook her head. No. Not possible. Not Carson. Not the other guys.

> These could be fake.

> Why would I fake them? What would I gain? Check the metadata yourself. They're real. I'm sorry, Ms. Crest. I know how much you care about your brother and the others.

Her fingers hovered over the keyboard.

> I need more proof before I believe this.

> Fair enough. But ask yourself, why is Astor suddenly so interested in protecting you? Is it because he cares... or because he's afraid of what you might discover?

Paisley slouched in the chair, frowning at her phone screen. Benedict had never shown interest in her before. At least not more than as her brother's best friend. Why now? Was it really about her safety, or was he monitoring her? Keeping her close to control what she learned?

No. She refused to believe it. She'd known Benedict for years. He wasn't capable of this.

But then, hadn't she thought the same about Carson?

She stared at her phone. If these documents were real, her brother and his friends, maybe even the man she loved, were criminals. If they were fake, someone was going to extraordinary lengths to frame them.

Either way, she was the only one who could find out the truth.

> Give me time. I need to verify these myself.

> Be careful who you trust. Especially Astor. Men like him are masters of manipulation.

She set down her phone on the table beside her laptop. The key he'd given her lay next to her empty coffee mug. He trusted her... or was it a clever way to keep her contained?

For the first time in her life, Paisley wasn't sure she knew her brother at all. And worse, the man she'd loved from afar for twelve years.

CHAPTER THREE

BENEDICT

BENEDICT'S MEETING WITH PENN HAD DRAGGED ON FOR hours. What should have been a straightforward discussion about upgrading their surveillance systems had spiraled into an intensive debate about encryption protocols and backdoor vulnerabilities. By the time he finally escaped, his head throbbed with technical jargon and his patience had worn thin.

All he wanted was to get home and check on Paisley.

The thought of her in his space had distracted him throughout the day. Penn had noticed his uncharacteristic lapses in attention, shooting him questioning glances when he'd asked Benedict the same question twice. Benedict had brushed it off as lack of sleep, but the truth was far more complicated.

Having Paisley in his home was like keeping a lit match next to gasoline. Dangerous. Potentially catastrophic. And yet, as he rode the elevator to his penthouse, anticipation hummed beneath his skin.

The moment he stepped inside, he knew something was wrong.

Paisley sat at his dining table, her laptop open before her, but her eyes were distant, unfocused. She startled when the door closed behind him, her hand instinctively covering her phone.

"Hey," she said, her voice too bright. Too forced. "How was your meeting?"

Benedict set his briefcase down, observing her with the practiced eye of someone who'd made a career of reading people. Her shoulders were tense, her smile didn't reach her eyes, and she was chewing the edge of her thumb.

"What happened?" he asked, ignoring her question.

She blinked. "What do you mean?"

"Something's wrong." He moved closer, noting how she shifted in her seat, angling her body to block her phone screen. "You're a terrible liar, Paisley."

"I'm not lying about anything." But her gaze dropped, unable to maintain eye contact.

Benedict unbuttoned his suit jacket and draped it over the back of a chair. "We had an agreement. If I'm going to help you, you need to be honest with me." He pulled out the chair across from her and sat down, resting his forearms on the table. "So I'll ask again: what happened while I was gone?"

For a moment, she looked like she might continue the charade. Then her shoulders slumped in defeat.

"My contact sent me something." She pushed her phone toward him, screen unlocked. "Audio files and financial records. They're... not good."

Benedict picked up the phone, scanning through the messages from someone listed simply as "M." His jaw tightened as he played the first audio file.

Carson's voice filled the space between them, discussing money transfers and shell companies. Then Tanner's voice. Then a mention of Penn.

As he listened to file after file, a cold fury built inside him. Not at Paisley for trying to hide this from him, but at whoever was orchestrating this elaborate frame.

"These are fake," he said when the last recording ended, setting the phone down.

"How can you be so sure?" Paisley's voice was small, uncertain.

"Because I know what we do and don't do at Crest Strategies." His gaze was steady on hers. "And money laundering for criminal clients isn't part of it."

"Then how do you explain the audio? The financial records with Carson's signature?"

"Technology is remarkably advanced these days." Benedict leaned back, his mind racing through possibilities. "Voice synthesis has reached the point where with enough sample material, anyone can be made to say anything. As for the financial records, Penn could forge those in his sleep, which means others with similar skills could as well."

"I want to believe you." She twisted her hands together. "But what if you're wrong? What if there's something happening that even you don't know about?"

The implication stung, but Benedict kept his expression neutral. "Who is 'M'?" he asked instead.

Paisley hesitated. "His name is Marcus. I met him at a fundraiser for my nonprofit a few months ago. He approached me with concerns about Crest Strategies."

"And you didn't think to tell Carson? Or me?" The hurt slipped into his voice despite his best efforts.

"I didn't know who to trust," she admitted. "And Marcus seemed so sincere, so concerned about potential victims."

"So concerned that he approached the sister of the supposed criminal mastermind?" Benedict shook his head. "That doesn't strike you as calculated?"

Paisley's eyes widened, the first crack in her certainty. "What are you saying?"

"I'm saying this isn't just about Carson anymore." Benedict stood and began to pace, his mind working through the implications. "This could be a coordinated attack on Crest Strategies as a whole. The mention of Penn and Tanner in those recordings? The financial records? Sounds like someone is trying to take us all down."

"But why? What could anyone gain from that?"

"Our client list includes some of the most powerful people in the country. People with secrets, enemies, vulnerabilities." Benedict stopped pacing and turned to face her. "If Crest Strategies falls, those secrets become leverage for whoever orchestrated our downfall."

Paisley pushed away from the table, standing to match his intensity. "So you're saying Marcus is using me to get to all of you? That this is all some elaborate scheme?"

"I'm saying we need to be extremely careful." Benedict stepped closer, close enough to catch the scent of his own soap on her skin; a detail that sent an inappropriate surge of possessiveness through him. "This Marcus clearly knows a lot about us. About you. He's been feeding you just enough information to make you doubt everything you know."

"Then prove him wrong." Her chin lifted in defiance. "Prove to me that Crest Strategies isn't involved in anything illegal."

Benedict studied her face. The challenge in her eyes, the stubborn set of her jaw. So like Carson. But there was vulnerability there too, a desperate hope that he was right.

"I'll do better than that," he said finally. "I'll help you uncover who's really behind this. But from now on, no more secrets between us. You tell me everything 'Marcus' sends you, immediately. And no more sneaking around Crest Strategies offices. We do this together or not at all."

Relief softened her features. "Deal." She extended her hand.

Benedict took it, ignoring the sensation that shot up his arm at the contact. Her hand was small in his, but her grip was firm. Trustworthy.

"First things first," he said, reluctantly releasing her hand. "We need to find out who Marcus really is. Send me everything you have on him. Descriptions, meeting locations, anything that might help identify him."

"I don't have much." She reached for her phone, scrolling through messages. "He always contacted me, never the other way around. Usually public places with lots of people."

"At least you never met him alone," Benedict muttered.

"I'm not an idiot. And I'm a single woman who lives in the city. I know how to stay out of the obituaries." She handed him her phone, showing a blurry photo of a man in a baseball cap and sunglasses. "This is the only picture I have. He didn't know I took it."

Benedict studied the image. Average height, nondescript features, nothing remarkable except the deliberate anonymity. This wasn't a concerned citizen reaching out to Paisley. This was someone with training.

"I'll have Penn run facial recognition," he said, forwarding the image to his secure server. At Paisley's alarmed expression, he added, "Discreetly. He won't know the context."

"Can you trust him?" she asked. "The audio mentioned Penn specifically."

"Which is exactly why I know it's fake." Benedict's voice softened. "Penn has the best heart out of all of us. The guy won't flush bugs down the toilet, let alone launder money to criminals who are doing far worse than creeping on the walls of the office."

Just as he'd said the words, his phone rang. The screen displayed Carson's name.

Benedict and Paisley exchanged a look before he answered. "Carson."

"We have a situation." Carson's voice was tight. "Someone hacked our client database. Sensitive information was accessed."

Benedict's gaze snapped to Paisley. "When?"

"Today. Penn just discovered the breach. He's tracing it now, but it looks professional. I need you back at the office."

"I'll be there in twenty." Benedict ended the call, his mind racing.

"What is it?" Paisley asked, concern etched across her face.

"Someone hacked Crest Strategies today." He grabbed his jacket. "The timing is too perfect to be a coincidence."

"You think it's connected to this? To Marcus?"

"I'd bet a couple billion on it." Benedict moved to the door, then paused. "Stay here. Don't contact Marcus. Don't leave the penthouse. Understood?"

Paisley nodded, her face pale. "Be careful, Ben."

The concern in her voice lingered with him as he rode the elevator down to the parking garage.

Benedict returned to his penthouse well after midnight, exhaustion etched into every line of his body. The hack had been sophisticated, bypassing security measures that Penn himself had designed. They'd spent hours tracing the breach, only to hit dead ends and false trails.

Whatever evidence they'd hoped to find had disappeared into the digital ether.

The penthouse was dark and quiet when he entered, only a small lamp left burning in the living room. Benedict loosened his tie, his thoughts still churning. The connection between the hack and the evidence Paisley had received seemed undeniable now. Someone was moving against Crest Strategies, likely with insider knowledge.

He poured himself two fingers of whiskey and downed it in one burning swallow.

"Ben?" Paisley's voice came from the hallway. She stood in the shadows, dressed in sleep shorts and a tank top, her dark hair loose around her shoulders. "What happened?"

Benedict set the glass down. "Professional job. They knew exactly what they were looking for and how to get it."

"Was anything taken?"

"Client information. Files. Nothing that should interest your friend Marcus, unless he's collecting blackmail material."

Paisley stepped into the light. "You think that's what this is about? Blackmail?"

"It's one possibility." Benedict moved to the couch and sat, running a hand through his hair. "Whoever's behind this has resources, technical skills, and a vendetta. They're playing a long game."

She crossed the room and sat beside him. "I'm sorry. I never meant to get caught in the middle of something like this."

"It's not your fault." He turned to face her. "You were manipulated by someone who knew exactly which buttons to push."

"My concern for Carson." She nodded. "My fear that he'd changed since Emma."

"And your natural desire to protect him." Benedict's voice softened. "The same way you've always looked out for him."

Paisley gave a hollow laugh. "Some protector I turned out to be. If you're right, I nearly helped destroy everything he's built. Everything *you've* built."

"You didn't know." Benedict hesitated, then reached out to tuck a stray curl behind her ear. The simple touch felt dangerously intimate in the dim light. "And now you'll help us find whoever's really behind this."

Her eyes locked with his. For a breathless moment, Benedict thought she might lean closer, erase the carefully maintained distance he'd kept for twelve years.

Instead, she stood abruptly. "You should get some rest. You look exhausted."

"I am." He stood as well, hyper-aware of how small she seemed in the vastness of his living room. How vulnerable. "But first, I need you to promise me something."

"What?"

"If Marcus contacts you again, tell me immediately. Don't respond, don't engage. Just tell me."

She nodded. "Okay."

"Good." He took a step back, creating necessary distance. "Goodnight, Pai."

"Night, Benny."

He watched her disappear down the hallway, fighting the urge to follow. To protect. To claim.

Benedict forced himself to walk to his own bedroom, closing the door behind him with a quiet click. He removed his tie, unbuttoned his shirt, letting the events of the day wash over him. Someone was targeting not just Carson, but all of them. Using Paisley as an unwitting accomplice. The thought twisted his stomach in knots.

He stepped into the shower, letting hot water sluice over tense muscles. As the steam enveloped him, his mind kept returning to Paisley. To the vulnerability in her eyes when she realized she might've been used. To the fierce determination that had replaced it.

To the way she'd looked standing in his hallway. Her soft curves and sleepy eyes.

Benedict turned the water to cold, cursing himself for the direction of his thoughts. She was Carson's sister. Off-limits. A line he'd never cross, no matter how much he wanted to.

After toweling off and pulling on a pair of sleep pants, he lay in bed staring at the ceiling, sleep eluding him despite his exhaustion. Every creak of the penthouse, every distant siren from the city below kept him alert, on edge. Benedict closed his eyes, willing sleep to come. Then, faintly, he heard it. A soft buzzing sound coming from the room next door.

His eyes snapped open.

No. Fuck no.

She was not... God, she was.

He tried to block out the noise, to ignore the images flooding his mind. But as the buzzing continued, his imagination ran wild. He pictured her sprawled out on the bed. Head thrown back. Eyes squeezed shut.

Why, oh why, had she brought a fucking vibrator to his apartment?

He should move away. Go to his office. Put on headphones. Anything to give her privacy.

Benedict shifted, growing hard despite his best efforts. He clenched his fists, nails digging into his palms. This was torture. Sweet, agonizing torture. Just another layer to the hell Paisley had locked him in from the moment they met. Fuck, she was the devil.

The buzzing stopped briefly, replaced by a soft moan that sent a jolt of desire through him.

Then...

"Benedict..."

Christ.

It was barely a whisper, but it echoed in his mind like she'd screamed it. His cock throbbed, straining against his sweatpants. He gritted his teeth, fighting the urge to touch himself.

"Ben..." she moaned again, her voice laced with desire.

Fuck. He couldn't take this.

If she was going to get off to the thought of him—let alone torture him by making noise in the room next door—it was only fair he got the same ending.

He shoved his hand into his sweatpants, wrapping his fingers around his shaft. He was rock hard already. Using the bead of pre-cum that had already formed, he spread it around with his thumb as lubricant. As he began to stroke himself, he stopped trying to push away the images of Paisley. She consumed his thoughts.

Paisley's full lips parted in pleasure. Her expressive eyes dark with desire. He pictured the way her breasts looked in the tight shirts she wore. Her long, tan legs. The curve of her ass. God, he'd give anything to fuck her in the ass. The freckles dusting her skin. The way her natural curls framed her face. What would it feel like to grab a fist of her hair as he took her from behind. He envisioned her loud laughter, transforming into moans as she screamed his name and came on his dick. Each stroke brought him closer, her phantom touch pushing him to the edge.

Her name was on his lips as he matched the rhythm of her moans.

The buzzing started again, louder this time. Benedict's grip tightened, his strokes growing faster, more urgent. Tension built, the pressure mounting. He bit down on his lip, stifling a groan.

Paisley's moans grew louder, her pleasure escalating. Desperation clung to her voice, a raw need that mirrored his own. He was close, so fucking close.

"Benedict," she cried out, her voice breaking as she reached her climax.

The sound of his name pushed him over the edge. Benedict came hard, his body convulsing with release. Pleasure crashed over him, leaving him breathless and spent.

For a moment, silence fell over the penthouse. Then, softly, he heard Paisley sigh, a contented sound that sent a shiver down his spine. He lay there, panting, his heart pounding in his chest. What the fuck had just happened?

Fuck.

Fucking fuck.

How did this woman have such a strong grip over him?

Not just a grip, a strangling chokehold that had made him make a mess inside his sweatpants.

Damn it.

Benedict swung his legs out of bed, padding quietly to the bathroom. He cleaned himself up, wanting nothing more than to walk out his door and show his best friend's sister how much better he fucked than a shitty vibrator.

But know. She'd probably be mortified he'd heard her and he'd go and ruin everything.

Nope. Best thing to do would be to somehow sell his soul to the sleep gods and try to go the rest of the night without dwelling on the fact that the woman he loved had orgasmed to the thought of him doing who-knew-what to her.

Back in bed, he stared at the ceiling, sleep even more evasive than before. His body was sated, but his mind was a whirlwind. He needed to put distance between them, to regain control of his feelings. But how could he, when she was so close, so vulnerable, so utterly irresistible?

What the hell was he supposed to do now?

CHAPTER FOUR

PAISLEY

Hot water cascaded down Paisley's back as she leaned against the shower wall, trying to wash away the memory of last night. Her fingers had trembled as they'd moved between her thighs, seeking release from twelve years of denied desire. The vibrator she'd packed had hummed her right to climax, and she'd bitten her lip to muffle her cries.

But Benedict's name had escaped anyway, too powerful to contain.

She closed her eyes, letting the water drum against her scalp. Had he heard her? The thought sent twin currents of mortification and arousal through her body. She'd waited until she heard his shower running, thinking the water would mask any noise, but he'd showered so quickly that she hadn't finished in time. What if his walls were thinner than she'd thought? What if he had picked up her breathless moans?

What if he'd heard his name on her lips as she'd come undone?

Paisley shut off the water with more force than necessary. This was ridiculous. She was a grown woman, staying in the home of her brother's best friend for protection, and instead of focusing on the potential very real danger from Marcus, she was obsessing over whether Benedict had heard her masturbate.

Her priorities definitely needed some readjusting.

She toweled off quickly, dressing in dark jeans and a simple blouse that her nonprofit colleagues would call her "game face" outfit. Professional, put-together, with just enough femininity to disarm. As she applied minimal makeup, she practiced her expression in the mirror. Neutral. Calm. Not at all like a woman who'd fantasized about her host the night before. Of his hands on her skin. His tongue on her clit. His dick in her pussy.

Fuck, she was wet again.

Whose shitty idea was it to live with the man she held secret feelings for?

Oh right.

It was Benedict Fucking Astor's idea.

The asshole.

When she emerged from the guest room, Benedict stood at the kitchen island reviewing something on his tablet, dressed in dark jeans and a navy henley that clung to his broad shoulders. The casual attire was so unlike his usual tailored suits that she paused, momentarily thrown.

"I made coffee," he said without looking up, his voice perfectly controlled. "We need to be out in twenty minutes."

Paisley's stomach dropped. He'd heard her. He must have. Why else would he be so formal, so distant?

"Out where?" She poured herself coffee, hoping the mug would hide the trembling of her hands.

"The office first." He finally glanced up, his ice-blue eyes giving nothing away. "Then to meet with Penn. I've been thinking about those audio files."

"Penn?" She took a careful sip, watching him over the rim. "Can we trust him if those audio files mentioned him?"

"That's exactly why I want to meet with him." Benedict closed his tablet. "The files are too perfect, too incriminating. If someone's trying to frame Crest Strategies, I want to understand how they're doing it."

Paisley nodded, grateful for the shift to business. "What's the plan?"

"We go to Penn's lab, not the main office. Fewer people, more secure." He finally looked at her properly, his gaze sweeping over her in a quick assessment. "You might want to grab a jacket. Penn keeps his workspace at subzero temperatures."

"Of course he does." She rolled her eyes, some of the tension dissipating. "Let me guess, better for the servers?"

"Something like that." The ghost of a smile touched Benedict's lips. "He claims humans are the biggest threat to his equipment. Too much heat, too many fingerprints."

"Sounds like Penn." Paisley finished her coffee, setting the mug in the sink. "I'll grab my jacket."

In her room, she retrieved her phone, frowning at the notification on the screen. Three missed calls from Marcus. A text had come through while she was in the shower.

> Time running out. Need to meet today. Urgent.

Her stomach clenched. She should tell Benedict immediately. That had been their agreement. But something held her back. What if Marcus really did have information that could help them? What if Benedict's loyalty to Carson and the others blinded him to possibilities she needed to consider?

Paisley chewed her thumbnail, debating. Before she could decide, another text appeared:

> They know you're with Astor. Not safe. Meet me at Riverside Park, 11AM, south entrance. Come alone or I can't help you.

She quickly pocketed the phone as footsteps approached her door.

"Ready?" Benedict asked, leaning against the doorframe.

"Almost." She grabbed her jacket, trying to appear casual. "Just checking emails from work."

His gaze lingered on her face a moment too long, and she

34

wondered if he could read the lie there. If his surveillance expertise extended to detecting the slight flutter of her eyelashes, the way she chewed the inside of her cheek.

"Everything okay?" he asked, voice neutral.

"Fine." She forced a smile. "Nonprofit drama. Nothing important."

Benedict nodded, though something in his expression suggested he wasn't entirely convinced. "The car is waiting downstairs. Private entrance."

Twenty minutes later, they pulled up to what appeared to be an abandoned warehouse in the West Village. No signage, no visible cameras, nothing to suggest it housed one of the most sophisticated technological operations in the city.

Benedict parked in an unmarked garage that opened automatically as they approached. "Penn's a bit... particular about visitors," he warned as the door closed behind them. "Try not to touch anything."

"I know Penn," Paisley reminded him. "I know all of my brother's asshole friends."

"Shit, thanks for that," Benedict said, rolling his eyes as he flashed her a grin. "But this is different. This is his sanctuary." Killing the engine, Benedict turned to face her. "The Penn at the office and at social events is a carefully constructed façade. The real Penn lives here, among his machines."

Paisley unbuckled her seatbelt. "You make him sound like some sort of shut-in who never showers and talks to computers like they're people."

"Pretty much. Although he did have a shower installed her, so more so the latter than the former. Come on."

As they approached a nondescript metal door, Paisley checked her watch again. 10:23 AM. She was running out of time if she was going to meet Marcus.

"I need to use the restroom," she said. "Is there one before we go in?"

Benedict turned, his gaze sweeping over her face. "There's one inside. Penn's quite proud of the Japanese toilet he imported. Self-heating seat, apparently."

"Of course he did. As if men need further reasons to sit on a toilet longer than they already do." She forced a laugh. "Lead the way."

Rather than the cold, sterile environment she'd imagined, Penn's lab was a riot of color and organized chaos. Screens covered nearly every wall, each displaying different data streams. Workstations cluttered with half-completed projects occupied the center of the room. And there, in the midst of it all, sat Penn himself, surrounded by at least eight monitors, his fingers flying across multiple keyboards.

"You're late," he called without looking up. "And you brought company."

"I told you I was bringing Paisley," Benedict said, guiding her further into the space with a light touch at her back.

"You did?" Penn finally swiveled in his chair, his expression surprised. "Must have been multitasking." His gaze landed on Paisley, a quick assessment that felt like being scanned. "Hi Paisley."

"Hey Penn."

Penn's attention had already shifted back to Benedict. "You said this was urgent. Something about the hack?"

"And more." Benedict moved to one of the workstations. "Where's that bathroom you're so proud of? She needs it."

"Down the hall, first door on the right. Don't touch the control panel unless you know what you're doing." Penn turned back to his screens. "Voice authentication enabled."

Paisley raised an eyebrow at Benedict, who shrugged as if to say, 'I warned you.'

She followed Penn's directions, closing the bathroom door behind her and immediately pulling out her phone. 10:31 AM. She texted Marcus:

> Running late. Can we make it 11:30?

His response came immediately:

> 11:15 latest. Critical information. Lives at stake.

Paisley bit her lip, calculating. If she could slip out now, she might make it by 11:15. But how? Benedict would notice her absence immediately, and she doubted she could just walk out the front door of Penn's fortress.

She used the bathroom quickly—the toilet was indeed impressive, though she had no time to appreciate its features—and splashed water on her face. As she dried her hands, she noticed a small window near the ceiling. It looked barely large enough for a person to squeeze through, but it might be her only option.

Paisley checked her phone again. 10:36 AM. She needed to decide now.

Taking a deep breath, she positioned one of the small decorative stools beneath the window and climbed up, testing whether it would open. To her surprise, it swung outward easily. She peered through to see an alley below. Not a far drop, maybe six feet.

This was madness. Climbing out a bathroom window to meet a mysterious contact who might be manipulating her? But what if Marcus really did have information that could help protect Carson? What if lives truly were at stake?

Decision made, Paisley hoisted herself up and through the window, landing with a soft thud in the alley below. She brushed herself off, oriented toward the street, and began walking.

CHAPTER FIVE

BENEDICT

BENEDICT KNEW SOMETHING WAS WRONG THE MOMENT Penn's security alert flashed on the nearest monitor.

"Someone just exited through the bathroom window," Penn announced, already pulling up camera feeds. "East alley."

Benedict was moving before Penn finished speaking, his heart rate accelerating. "Show me."

The security footage revealed exactly what he feared: Paisley, climbing out the window, checking her phone before hurrying away.

"She has to be meeting him," Benedict said, his voice tight. "Can you access her phone remotely?"

Penn's fingers flew across his keyboard. "Already on it. You said it might be compromised when you messaged earlier." A few seconds of intense typing, then: "Got it. Text messages coming through now."

Benedict leaned over Penn's shoulder, reading the exchange between Paisley and Marcus. *Riverside Park. 11:15. Lives at stake.*

"Looks like she got a taxi according to the latest text." Penn nodded towards a screen to his left. "She'll be at the park soon."

"She's walking into a trap," he said, already heading for the door.

"Benedict," Penn's voice stopped him. "I ran that photo through facial recognition while you were driving over. His name isn't Marcus."

Benedict turned, his hand on the doorknob. "Who?"

"Dawson Flintly."

"Are you sure?"

"Positive." Penn's expression was grim. "Looks different now. Lost weight, changed his hair. But it's him."

"Fuck."

Dawson Flintly, a man Benedict had personally caught selling client information seven years ago, had been fired immediately. Not only that, Carson had taken Benedict's suggestion and had subsequently blacklisted Flintly in the industry. The man who'd sworn revenge as security had escorted him from the building.

"He's working for Blackwater now," Penn added. "Senior partner, according to their website."

"How in the hell did he get a job with…never mind. Track Paisley's phone," Benedict ordered, already moving. "Keep me updated on her location." He tried calling Paisley as he left the warehouse, but it went to voicemail.

As he sprinted to his car, his phone buzzed with a text from Penn:

> She's heading uptown. ETA Riverside Park 11:12.

Benedict started the engine, his mind already mapping the fastest route. Traffic would be a nightmare, but he knew shortcuts most drivers didn't.

Anger and concern battled for dominance as he navigated through the city. Why hadn't she trusted him? After bringing her into his home? After promising to tell him when Marcus tried to contact her, why go behind his back?

Shit.

He knew why.

He'd never given her reason to believe he saw her as an equal; as anything more than Carson's little sister who needed protection.

Benedict pushed the thought aside, focusing on the road. There would be time for self-recrimination later. Right now, he needed to reach Paisley before Flintly did.

His phone buzzed again:

> Taxi dropped her at Riverside Park south entrance. 11:09.

Benedict was still at least five minutes away. Too slow. He needed to warn her.

He pulled over long enough to send a text:

> It's a trap, Paisley. "Marcus" is Dawson Flintly, former Crest employee. Dangerous. Wait for me.

As he hit send, he watched the message status: Delivered. Read.

No response.

He tried calling again.

She didn't answer.

Benedict cursed, pulling back into traffic. She was ignoring him, believing whatever story Flintly had fed her over the past months. The manipulation had been thorough, professional. Personal.

By some miracle of aggressive driving and a few traffic laws bent beyond recognition, Benedict pulled up to Riverside Park at 11:13. He parked illegally on the street, scanning the south entrance. No sign of Paisley.

A text from Penn guided him.

> Her phone shows she's heading toward the river overlook. 200 yards from south entrance.

Benedict moved quickly through the park, keeping to the treeline for cover. Morning joggers and dog walkers paid him no attention as he scanned the paths ahead, looking for Paisley's familiar figure.

He spotted her near the water, alone, checking her watch anxiously. Relief flooded him. He'd beaten Flintly to the meeting. Without hesitation, Benedict approached her from behind, catching her elbow just as she turned.

"Ben!" She jumped, startled by his sudden appearance. "What the hell—"

"We're leaving." His voice left no room for argument as he guided her firmly toward the exit. "Now."

"Let go of me." Paisley pulled her arm free, stepping back. "I'm meeting someone."

"You're meeting Dawson Flintly, a former Crest Strategies employee who was fired for selling client information." Benedict kept his voice low, aware of people nearby. "A man who now works for our biggest competitor and has apparently spent years plotting revenge."

Paisley's eyes widened, but her chin lifted in that stubborn way that was so quintessentially her. "I want to hear what he has to say."

"No, you don't." Benedict took her arm again, gentler this time. "Whatever he's told you has been carefully crafted to manipulate you. To use you against us."

"And I'm just supposed to take your word for it?" Anger flashed in her eyes.

"Yes." His patience snapped. "Because unlike Flintly, I've spent twelve years protecting you, not using you."

Paisley opened her mouth to argue, but Benedict's attention had shifted to something over her shoulder. A man had entered the park from the south entrance; average height, expensive casual clothes, hair different from the photo but undeniably Dawson Flintly.

"Time's up," Benedict muttered, taking Paisley's hand firmly in his. "We're going."

This time he didn't give her a choice, pulling her along a path that would keep them hidden from Flintly's view. To his surprise, she followed without further protest, though the tension in her body told him this was far from over.

They reached his car without incident, and Benedict opened the passenger door. "Get in."

"I'm not a child, Benedict." But she slid into the seat, her movements rigid.

Benedict circled to the driver's side, starting the engine and pulling away from the curb just as Flintly appeared at the park entrance, scanning the area with obvious frustration.

For several blocks, they drove in tense silence. Benedict kept checking the rearview mirror, ensuring they weren't followed, while Paisley stared resolutely out the passenger window.

"You had no right," she finally said, her voice tight.

"I had every right." Benedict's grip tightened on the steering wheel. "You were walking into a trap laid by a man who's spent years planning revenge against Crest Strategies."

"So you say." She turned to face him. "But all I have is your word against his. And honestly, Ben, you say that everything he's sent me has been fake, but you haven't proven any of it. What if it is real? What if you're lying to me?"

The accusation stung more than it should have. "What exactly have I lied to you about?"

"How am I supposed to know?" Her voice rose. "You and Carson and all the other guys just see me as some little girl who tags along sometimes. You all make decisions for me, treat me like I'm some fragile doll who can't deal with all the things you deal with."

"Where is this even coming from?"

"It doesn't matter. The point is, Marcus—"

"Flintly."

"Shut up. The point is, he trusted me to do this. All you five seem to see in me is some little sister who throws parties for rich people. You don't see how capable I am."

"That's not true at all. I—"

"You're the worst of them! At least Carson has a reason for treating me this way. He's my brother. What's your excuse?"

"I've been trying to protect you!"

"I don't need your protection!" Paisley's hands clenched in her lap. "I need your respect. I need you to see me as an equal, not as some responsibility you've been saddled with."

Benedict abruptly pulled off onto a side street, parking the car with a jerk. He turned to face her fully, his composure fracturing.

"You think that's what this is? Some obligation?" His voice had dropped dangerously low. "You think I'm following Carson's orders to keep an eye on his little sister?"

"Aren't you?" She met his gaze. "Isn't that what I've always been to all of you? Carson's kid sister who needs protecting?"

"For fuck's sake, Paisley." Benedict ran a hand through his hair. "If that were true, don't you think I'd have told Carson about any of this? About Flintly, or the files, or you sneaking around his office?"

That gave her pause. "Why haven't you?"

"Because I know how he'd react. Because I wanted to give you the chance to figure this out without him swooping in and taking over." Benedict's gaze held hers. "Because I respect you enough to let you make your own choices, even when those choices terrify me."

"Like meeting with Marcus—with Flintly," she corrected herself.

"Yes." His jaw tightened. "Even though every instinct I have was screaming to lock you away somewhere safe."

Paisley studied his face, confusion replacing some of the anger. "Why do you care so much, Ben? Why go to all this trouble for me specifically?"

"Because it's you!" The words exploded from him. "Because for twelve years, I've been watching you, protecting you, keeping my distance because you're Carson's sister and my business partner's sister and the one goddamn person in this world I can't have!"

Benedict's chest heaved. Paisley stared at him, shock written across her features.

"What are you saying?" she whispered.

"I'm saying that I know your daily routines. I know which coffee shop you visit every Tuesday morning. I know you take the long way home on Fridays to stop at that little bookstore on 12th." His voice roughened. "Not because I'm stalking you, but because I can't help noticing everything about you."

Paisley's lips parted, but no sound emerged. Benedict turned away, unable to face the rejection he was certain would follow his confession.

"Why the hell do you even care?" she finally managed, her voice barely audible.

"Doesn't matter."

"Why, Benedict?"

"Paisley, just drop it."

"Fuck that. Tell me why."

Benedict's hands clenched on the steering wheel, his knuckles white. When he turned back to her, his expression was stripped bare of all pretense.

"Because I've been in love with you since the moment we met," he said, voice hoarse. "And I've spent every day since trying to pretend I'm not."

CHAPTER SIX

BENEDICT

Benedict hadn't meant to confess.

Twelve years of careful restraint, of maintaining distance, of redirecting his thoughts whenever they strayed to dangerous territory—all undone in a moment of raw frustration.

He stared straight ahead, unable to look at Paisley. His pulse hammered against his ribs as he waited for her reaction. Disgust, perhaps. Or worse, pity. The poor, obsessed man who'd spent over a decade pining for his best friend's little sister.

"Look at me, Ben."

He couldn't. If he turned, if he saw rejection in those eyes he'd memorized years ago, something in him would break beyond repair.

"Benedict." Her voice was soft. "Look at me."

Slowly, he turned.

He hadn't expected the flush across her cheekbones, the rapid rise and fall of her chest, the searing heat in her gaze.

"Say it again," she whispered.

Benedict swallowed, his throat dry. "Which part?"

"The part where you've been in love with me for twelve years."

His hands throttled the steering wheel. "I've been in love with you since the moment you hugged me at Carson's birthday and told me any friend of his was family to you." The confession came easier the second time. "I've spent every day since convincing myself to stay away."

"Because of Carson." It wasn't a question.

"Because of Carson. Because you're his little sister and he deemed you off limits to all of us. Because of a thousand reasons that seemed important at the time." His voice roughened. "Because I was afraid you'd never see me as anything more than your brother's friend."

"Fuck Carson."

"Thanks, but I'd rather not."

Paisley's laugh was soft. "Ben, I've been in love with you since I was eighteen."

The words didn't register at first. When they did, he could've sworn his heart stopped beating.

"What?" He couldn't have heard her correctly.

"I've been in love with you since I was eighteen." Paisley's eyes held his, unwavering despite the vulnerability in her expression. "That same day. Twelve years, Benedict. Twelve years of watching you from across rooms, of making excuses to visit Carson's office just to see you, of dating men who never measured up because none of them were you."

Benedict's world tilted on its axis. Every interaction, every lingering glance he'd dismissed as his imagination, every moment he'd convinced himself she couldn't possibly feel the same—all rewritten in an instant.

"Paisley," he whispered.

"Last night," she continued, a hint of defiance in her voice, "In the guest room, I—"

"I heard." Heat flooded his face. "I mean, I didn't intend to listen. I would never—"

"I was thinking of you. I always think of you."

Something inside Benedict snapped. Twelve years of control, of distance, of denial. Gone in an instant.

He moved without conscious thought, releasing his seatbelt and closing the distance between them. His hand cupped the back of her neck, fingers tangling in her hair as he pulled her toward him.

"Tell me to stop," he murmured, his lips a breath away from hers.

"Don't you dare," she whispered back.

Their mouths crashed together, the kiss nothing like the restrained, polite first encounter he'd imagined. This was raw, desperate, years of pent-up longing unleashed at once. Paisley made a sound, half gasp, half moan, that sent fire through his veins. Her hands clutched at his shoulders, nails digging through the fabric of his shirt as she tried to pull him closer despite the awkward angle.

Benedict's mind went blank, years of hyperawareness narrowing to a single point of focus: Paisley's mouth under his, her tongue sliding against his own, the taste of her more intoxicating than any whiskey.

He pulled back just enough to look at her. Flushed cheeks, parted lips, eyes dark with desire. His Paisley. Finally his.

"God, I wanted this. Wanted you," he said.

"I've always been yours." She pulled him back to her, the kiss deeper this time, more deliberate.

The center console dug into his ribs as he leaned across it. With a growl of frustration, Benedict pulled back, glancing around. They were parked on a quiet side street, relatively secluded, but still in broad daylight.

"We should—" he began.

"I will murder you if you end this," Paisley interrupted, her fingers curling into his shirt.

"I was going to say we should find somewhere more private." He brushed his thumb across her lower lip, satisfaction surging through him when she shivered at the contact. "But I'm not sure I can wait that long."

Twelve years of fantasies, of denied need, of wanting, all crystallizing into an urgent hunger that demanded immediate satisfaction.

Paisley's eyes darkened further. "Then don't wait."

The words shattered what remained of his control. Benedict scanned the street once more—habit, training, the surveillance expert never fully dormant—before making a decision.

"Backseat," he ordered, his voice dropping to a register he barely recognized. "Now."

He didn't wait for her response, exiting the driver's side and circling to the rear door. Paisley was already climbing over the center console, her movements less graceful but just as urgent.

Benedict slid into the backseat after her, closing the door and engaging the privacy locks. The windows were tinted, the space confined but secluded enough. He turned to find Paisley already reaching for him, and then she was in his lap, straddling him, her weight a delicious pressure against his growing hardness.

"Twelve years," she murmured against his mouth between kisses. "Twelve fucking years of wanting this."

"Every day," he agreed, his hands sliding under her blouse to find warm skin. "Every moment."

The revelation that she'd wanted him too fueled his desire to a fever pitch. His fingers traced up her spine, cataloging each vertebra, committing the feel of her to memory in case this moment proved to be nothing more than another elaborate fantasy.

Paisley arched into his touch, her head falling back to expose the elegant line of her throat. Benedict couldn't resist trailing his lips along that column of skin, tasting her pulse point, breathing in the scent of her shampoo; the same one he'd caught hints of for years across conference tables and crowded rooms.

"Off, now," she ordered, tugging at his henley.

Benedict chuckled against her skin. "Demanding. I like it."

He helped her pull the shirt over his head, watching her eyes widen as she took in his bare chest, her fingers immediately tracing the wolf tattoo that curled around his left shoulder, down his biceps, and over his back.

"I've dreamed about touching this," she admitted, following the lines of ink with her fingertips. "Ever since that first beach day years ago."

The memory made him harder as he remembered Paisley in a navy bikini, hair wild from the salt air, freckles scattered across her nose from the sun. He'd gone swimming to hide his body's response to the sight of her, to douse the flames before Carson or anyone else noticed.

"I went in the water that day to hide how much I wanted you," he confessed, hands sliding up her sides, bringing her blouse with them. "How close I was to forgetting every promise I'd made to your brother."

Paisley raised her arms, allowing him to pull the garment over her head. She sat before him in a simple black bra, nothing elaborate but somehow more erotic than any lingerie could have been. Perhaps because it was her. Because it was real.

"What promises?" she asked, reaching behind to unclasp her bra.

Benedict's brain short-circuited as the material fell away, revealing perfect breasts with dusky pink nipples already tightened with arousal. Reality put every fantasy he'd imagined to shame.

"To protect you," he managed, his hands moving to cup the weight of her breasts, thumbs brushing over sensitive peaks. "To keep you safe. To never...ah, fuck...to never cross this line."

Paisley's eyes fluttered closed as he touched her, a soft moan escaping her lips. "Carson doesn't control me," she said, echoing words she'd spoken before. "Or my heart."

"Or this." Benedict leaned forward, taking one nipple into his mouth, savoring her sharp intake of breath, the way her fingers clutched at his shoulders.

He lavished attention on her breasts, alternating between gentle kisses and more demanding suction, learning what made her gasp, what made her arch against him. All the while, his hands explored. The curve of her waist, the flare of her hips, the perfect roundness of her ass as she ground against his erection.

"Ben," she breathed, her movements growing more urgent. "Please."

The plea in her voice nearly undid him. Benedict had always prided himself on control, on patience, on meticulous planning. But with Paisley writhing in his lap, years of denied desire demanded satisfaction.

His hands moved to the button of her jeans, pausing there. "Are you sure?" he asked, needing to hear it explicitly despite the evidence of her desire.

"I've never been more sure of anything," Paisley answered, her gaze meeting his with absolute certainty. "I want you, Benedict. I've always wanted you."

Permission granted, he made quick work of her jeans, helping her shimmy out of them in the confined space of the backseat. The sight of her in nothing but black panties, straddling his lap with kiss-swollen lips and disheveled hair, was almost enough to make him come undone then and there.

"You're beautiful," he murmured, running his hands up her thighs. "Even more beautiful than I imagined."

A flush spread across her chest at his words. "You've imagined this?"

"More times than I can count." His fingers traced the edge of her panties, feeling the dampness there. "Late at night. In meetings when you'd stop by Carson's office. Every time I saw you across a room and couldn't have you."

Her hips bucked as his fingers slipped beneath the fabric, finding her soaked. "Oh god, Ben."

"I've thought about how you'd feel," he continued, circling her clit with just enough pressure to drive her higher. "How you'd taste. How you'd sound when you came."

Paisley's head fell forward onto his shoulder, her breath hot against his skin as his fingers explored. "Like—fuck—like last night?"

The reminder that he'd heard her pleasure herself while thinking of him sent a fresh surge of arousal through him. His jeans were too tight against his straining cock. "Yes," he admitted. "You made a mess out of my sweat pants, moaning like that."

"I thought you might have heard." Her voice was breathless as his finger slid inside her, curling to find the spot that made her gasp. "P-part of me w-wanted you to." She clenched around him, and he tightened his grip on her ass with his other hand.

"I considered coming to you," he confessed, adding a second finger, feeling her stretch around him. God, she was so tight and so wet. "Almost broke down that door and replaced your toy with my tongue."

Paisley moaned, rocking against his hand. "Next time," she promised. "Right now I need you inside me."

Benedict withdrew his fingers, ignoring her whimper of protest. "Condom in my wallet," he explained. She shifted off him so he could grab his wallet from the front cup holder. He sat back down with wallet in hand, pulling out the wrapped package.

"You came prepared," she teased climbing back on top of him. Her fingers worked at his belt, unlatching it. She unbuttoned the jeans and he groaned with relief.

"Boy scout." The joke fell flat as her hand brushed against his erection, still confined in his boxers. "Fuck, Pai." He lifted her with his hips, and she helped him shimmy out of his jeans. Next came the boxers.

When Paisley's gaze landed on his fully hard dick, her eyes widened. "Definitely not a boy scout," she murmured, leaning forward to press a kiss to his neck as she stroked him.

Benedict's eyes rolled back at the sensation of her hand around him. How many nights had he lain awake imagining exactly this? How many cold showers had he taken to banish thoughts of Paisley touching him?

She pulled back, pupils fully dilated. "I'm clean. Got tested a few months ago. You?"

Benedict blinked, the question catching him off guard. "Yes, I'm clean too. But with the condom—"

Paisley answered by shifting off his lap, settling onto the seat beside him. Her hand wrapped around his cock, stroking up and down with enough of a twist to have him thrusting upwards into her hand. Benedict's breath hitched, his body tensing as pleasure shot through him.

"What are you—"

His words cut off with a groan as she leaned down, her tongue tracing the length of him. Every muscle in his body went rigid, his mind blanking as she took him into her mouth. The sensation was overwhelming, the warmth and wetness of her mouth, the feel of her tongue swirling around him.

"Fuck, Pai," he breathed, his hand reaching out to grip her hair, not to guide her but to anchor himself. His world narrowed down to the sight of her lips around him, the feel of her mouth working him closer and closer to the edge.

She used her tongue and lips, taking him deep despite the awkward angle. For a second, she choked, gagging. But she went back down even further than before. Benedict's heart pounded in his chest, his breath turning into nothing but ragged gasps. He was spiraling, the sensation too intense, too consuming. He was going to come undone, and it was all because of Paisley.

He realized almost too late that he was about to lose control.

"Paisley, stop," he gasped, his hands trembling as he gently pushed her away. "I can't—not yet."

She looked up at him, her eyes glazed over, her lips wet and swollen. The sight of her like that almost had him finishing without her mouth on him.

"Okay," she whispered, her voice husky with need.

Benedict shook with the effort to hold back. "I need to be inside you," he said, his voice rough with desire. "I need to feel you around me when I come."

With trembling hands, he took the forgotten condom, tearing the packet open and rolling it on. Paisley watched with hooded eyes, her bottom lip caught between her teeth.

"God, you're perfect" she whispered, positioning herself above him. "Fuck me."

Benedict guided her hips, the head of his cock pressing against her entrance. "Slowly," he cautioned, though every instinct screamed at him to thrust upward. "It's been a while for me and you nearly had me a second ago. I want this to be good for you. I want it to last." Benedict leaned forward and kissed her, letting the head of his dick rub her clit. She jerked at the touch, but kissed him back.

"Me too," she admitted, finally sinking down inch by torturous inch. "No one else has felt right since I realized it was always you."

The exquisite pressure of her body accepting his, nearly had him coming again. God, he needed to think of something—anything—else, or this would be the most embarrassing two seconds of his fucking life. Benedict gritted his teeth, fighting for control as Paisley settled fully onto him, her inner walls gripping him.

"Fuck," he breathed, resting his forehead against hers. "You feel perfect."

For a moment, neither moved, both adjusting to the overwhelming sensation of being joined after so many years of longing. Then Paisley rolled her hips, and Benedict's hands tightened on her waist.

"Fuck, shit, yes," he encouraged, guiding her movements to make sure she moved slowly. "Just like that."

She set a rhythm, rising and falling on him, her hands braced on his shoulders for leverage. Benedict matched her movements, thrusting upward when she came down, creating a friction that had them both gasping.

"You're so beautiful," he murmured, one hand sliding up to cup her breast, thumb circling her nipple. "So fucking perfect."

Benedict fought a losing battle with his body, every nerve ending sparking with the need for release. Paisley's rhythm faltered as she chased her own pleasure, her hips moving erratically, driving him closer to the edge.

"Slow down, Pai," he gritted out, his hands gripping her hips tighter. "A little longer."

But Paisley was lost in sensation, her head thrown back, eyes closed. She didn't slow down; she sped up, her body slamming down onto his. Benedict groaned, his control slipping.

"Fuck, Paisley, slow down," he growled, but she didn't. Desperate, he grabbed her hips and forced her down onto him, impaling her completely. She gasped, her eyes flying open, meeting his gaze.

"Ben," she whimpered, trying to move, but he held her firmly in place.

"Don't move," he ordered, his voice rough. "Just—give me a second."

But neither could stay still. Their bodies writhed together, desperate for friction, for the release that hovered just out of reach. She clenched her inner muscles around him, hot and wet and pulsing with need.

With a growl, he gave up the fight. His hands tightened on her hips as he pulled out and thrust upward, hard and deep. Paisley cried out, her fingers digging into his shoulders as she met his thrusts with her own, their bodies slamming together.

The sound of their flesh meeting filled the car. Paisley moaned his name in his ear, begging him not to stop. Benedict's world narrowed down to the feel of Paisley around him, the sight of her above him, her breasts bouncing with each thrust, her head thrown back in ecstasy.

She started to tighten around him, her body trembling as she neared her orgasm. He shifted his angle, pumping into her, chasing her release as much as his own. Their bodies were slick with sweat, their breaths ragged and syncopated.

"Close," Paisley gasped, her nails digging into his skin. "So fucking close, Ben. Don't fucking...fuck...don't fucking stop."

Benedict redoubled his efforts, his body slamming into hers with a force that shook the car. His own orgasm built, his body tensing as he fought to hold back until she came.

"Come on, Pai," he growled, his voice barely recognizable. "I want you to come first."

Paisley's pace quickened, her movements growing erratic. She swore over and over in his ear as she bent over him. He shifted again, changing the angle to hit the spot that made her cry out.

"That's it," he encouraged, voice rough with need. "Come on baby."

He rubbed her clit with his thumb, circling in time with their thrusts. Paisley's nails dug into his shoulders, leaving deep scratches he would happily tattoo into his skin.

"Ben, I, fuck, Ben—" His name was a broken cry on her lips as she shattered, her inner walls pulsing around him, drawing him deeper.

The sight of her coming undone—flushed cheeks, parted lips, eyes closed—combined with the physical sensation pushed Benedict over the edge. His hips jerked upward as his own release tore through him, more intense than any orgasm he'd experienced before.

"Paisley," he groaned, pulling her against him as the aftershocks rippled through them both. "My Paisley."

They remained locked together, breathing gradually slowing, hearts returning to normal rhythm. Benedict pressed gentle kisses to her shoulder, her neck, the curve of her jaw, unwilling to separate from her just yet.

Finally, Paisley lifted her head from where it had rested against his shoulder, meeting his gaze with a mixture of satisfaction and vulnerability.

"That was..." she began.

"Worth the twelve-year wait?" he suggested, tucking a stray curl behind her ear.

Her smile was radiant. "I was going to say 'just the beginning,' but yes, definitely worth the wait."

Something possessive and fierce surged through Benedict at her words. Just the beginning. Not a one-time release of tension, not a mistake to be regretted, but the start of something he'd denied himself for too long.

"I should have told you years ago," he said, tracing the line of her jaw with his thumb. "Wasted so much time."

"Oh, I have a feeling we'll make up for it." Paisley leaned into his touch. "That's what matters."

"Yeah," he kissed her collar bone. "You're absolutely right."

CHAPTER SEVEN

PAISLEY

Paisley's back pressed against the cold marble of Benedict's kitchen counter. His hands gripped her thighs, spreading them wider as he thrust into her with an intensity that stole her breath.

"God, Ben," she gasped, fingers tangling in his hair as he leaned forward to capture her mouth in a bruising kiss.

The moment they'd returned to his penthouse, they'd barely made it through the door before desperation overtook them. Clothes left a trail from the entryway to the kitchen. Her blouse draped over a barstool, his jeans abandoned by the refrigerator, her bra hanging precariously from a cabinet handle.

Twelve years of wanting, of waiting, had created a hunger that couldn't be satisfied with just one encounter in his car.

Benedict broke the kiss, his forehead resting against hers, his breathing ragged. "This is what I want to do for the rest of my fucking life," he murmured, one hand sliding up to cup her breast, thumb circling her nipple in a way that made her arch against him. "So fucking perfect."

The profanity in his normally controlled voice sent heat spiraling through her. This was a side of Benedict she'd never seen before. God, she loved it. The careful composure that defined him in public had crumbled completely, leaving something primal and possessive in its place. And fuck, she wanted him to possess every single part of her.

"Fuck, I agree," she admitted, her voice breaking as he hit a spot inside her that made stars explode behind her eyes. "And once your done taking me in your kitchen. I want you to fuck me on your couch. Against every wall of your apartment. On the floor. In the chair. On the fucking laundry machine. I want you to…fuckkk."

A growl rumbled in his chest, his rhythm faltering briefly before intensifying. "Tell me more," he demanded, his voice rough with need. "Tell me everything you've imagined."

"You bending me over your desk at the office," she continued, emboldened by the way his eyes darkened at her words. "Making me come while the others are just outside the door."

Benedict's grip on her thighs tightened, leaving marks she knew would bloom into bruises by morning. Marks she would press on to feel the sting, to remind herself it wasn't just another elaborate fantasy.

"What else?" he pressed, his movements growing more urgent.

"The shower," she gasped, feeling the familiar tension building inside her. "You pinning me against the tile, taking me from behind while the water runs over us."

"We'll do that next," he promised, the simple declaration sending a fresh wave of arousal through her. "After I make you come right here."

His hand slid between their bodies. The dual sensation of his cock filling her and his fingers circling her clit pushed Paisley to the edge faster than she'd thought possible.

"Ben," she whimpered, nails digging into his shoulders. "I'm going to—"

"Now," he commanded, his gaze locked with hers. "Do it now."

The intensity in his ice-blue eyes, the possessive edge to his voice, the way he seemed to know exactly how to touch her. It was all too much. Paisley's climax swept over her in surges, her body clenching around him as pleasure obliterated every thought except his name, which she cried out without restraint.

Benedict followed moments later, his release triggered by the pulsing of her inner walls. His hips jerked against hers as he emptied himself inside the condom they'd nearly forgotten to use.

For several minutes, they remained locked together, hearts racing in tandem, breath mingling in the space between them. Benedict's hands gentled, one moving to stroke her hair, the other drawing lazy patterns on her hip.

"You are almost too good at that." She grinned up at him, running her fingers through his sandy blonde hair, which stuck to his forehead in places from the sweat.

"I'm glad your satisfied," he said, pressing a soft kiss to her forehead.

"For now, at least. Give it a couple minutes and I'll be ready for that shower you promised me."

Benedict carefully withdrew from her, supporting her as she slid off the counter on unsteady legs.

"Good?"

"Perfect." She wrapped her arms around his neck, pulling him down for a kiss.

"Come on," he said, taking her hand and leading her toward the living room. "We should talk before that shower."

Paisley glanced at their scattered clothing, aware of her nakedness. Benedict seemed to sense her discomfort, because he released her hand long enough to retrieve his discarded button-down from the floor, handing it to her with a small smile.

"Thank you," she said, slipping it on. The shirt hung to mid-thigh, engulfing her in fabric that carried his scent.

In the living room, they settled onto his plush sofa, Paisley curling into his side as if they'd been doing this for years instead of a couple hours. Benedict, still gloriously naked, draped an arm around her shoulders, his fingers absently playing with a strand of her hair.

"We should discuss Flintly," he said after a moment of comfortable silence.

Shit.

The past few hours had created a bubble where only they existed. She liked that bubble. Stupid bastard had to pop it.

"What do you think he'll do next?" she asked, shifting to look at him.

Benedict's expression darkened. "He'll likely figure out you don't trust him. Adjust his strategy now that his cover is blown. The question is whether he'll escalate or retreat."

"You don't think he'll give up?"

"No." The certainty in Benedict's voice sent a chill through her. "Penn is looking into it, but it looks like he's been planning this for years. He built his career at Blackwater by promising to destroy Crest Strategies."

"Blackwater?" The name was vaguely familiar. "Your competitor?"

"More than competitors. They're our shadows. Everything we refuse to be. Where we draw lines, they cross them. Where we maintain ethical boundaries for most cases, they bulldoze through them." Benedict's jaw tightened. "And they've been trying to poach our clients and steal our methods since we opened our doors."

Paisley frowned. "So Flintly—"

"Found the perfect home for his vendetta," Benedict finished. "He was an analyst for us, brilliant with numbers but sloppy with security. I caught him selling client information."

"You fired him?"

"Cars and I did worse than fire him." A dangerous edge crept into Benedict's voice. "I made sure he couldn't work in reputation management again. At least, that's what I thought. Blackwater must have seen an opportunity; someone with inside knowledge of our operations and a personal grudge."

"And they've been using him to target you ever since," Paisley concluded. "Using me to get to Carson and the company."

Benedict nodded, his expression grim. "Flintly knows our weak points. He likely knows I—" He stopped, recalibrating. "He knows the importance of family to Carson. And he guessed that you'd do anything to protect your brother."

Paisley's stomach tightened. "I played right into his hands, didn't

I? Sneaking around Carson's office, taking photos of confidential files."

"You didn't know." Benedict's arm tightened around her shoulders. "Flintly is manipulative, and he's had years to perfect his approach. To study you, to figure out exactly which buttons to push."

The thought that someone had been watching her, analyzing her, for months or even years made Paisley's skin crawl. She'd felt strange when she discovered Benedict's surveillance, but at least his intentions had been protective. Flintly's were purely destructive.

"What now?" she asked, her hand absently tracing patterns on Benedict's chest, finding comfort in the steady beat of his heart beneath her fingers.

"Now we go on the offensive." His voice hardened. "Penn is tracking Flintly's digital footprint, trying to determine how deeply he's infiltrated our systems. Once we know the extent of the breach, we can seal it and start laying our own traps."

"And in the meantime?"

Benedict's hand moved to cup her face, tilting it up to meet his gaze. "In the meantime, you stay close to me. No wandering off, no meeting strangers in parks, no climbing out of bathroom windows."

Despite the seriousness of the situation, Paisley's lips curve into a smile. "You're never going to let me forget that, are you?"

"Not a chance." His thumb stroked her cheekbone. "You scared years off my life, Paisley."

Something in his tone made her heart skip. "I'm sorry," she said softly. "I thought I was helping."

"I know." He pressed a gentle kiss to her forehead. "But from now on, we do this together. No more secrets between us."

Paisley took a deep breath. "Speaking of secrets... what are we going to tell Carson?"

Benedict stiffened, but his arms remained around her. "That depends," he said carefully. "What do you want to tell him?"

"The truth, eventually." Paisley sat up straighter, needing to see his face clearly for this conversation. "But maybe not right away. Not while we're dealing with Flintly and Blackwater."

Relief flickered across Benedict's features. "I agree. Cars would be... distracted by our relationship. It would complicate an already complex situation."

"Plus, he might actually murder you," Paisley pointed out, only half joking.

"There is that possibility." Benedict's lips twitched. "Though I'd like to think twelve years of friendship would count for something."

"You fucked his little sister," she reminded him, her cheeks warming at the memory. "Twice in one day, in fact. Friendship might not be enough to save you."

"You're right." Benedict's laugh was low and warm. "Especially since I'm thinking the actual number of times I'll fuck you will be closer to six or seven times by the end of the day."

Fuck, the man had somehow found the exact button to make her wet. She was going to be walking around with her thighs clenched for the foreseeable future, it would seem.

"So we keep us a secret for now," she said, trying to redirect the conversation "Focus on getting rid of Flintly first, then deal with the Carson situation."

"Agreed." Benedict tucked a strand of hair behind her ear, his touch lingering. "Though keeping my hands off you in public might prove challenging."

"You managed it for twelve years," she teased.

"And it nearly killed me." His expression turned serious. "I don't want to hide how I feel about you. Not anymore. But I understand the need for discretion right now."

The vulnerability in his eyes made her throat tighten. This was a side of Benedict she'd only glimpsed in rare, unguarded moments over the years. The man beneath the carefully constructed exterior. The man who felt deeply, who loved fiercely, who protected what was his without hesitation.

"We'll figure it out," she promised, resting her hand over his heart.

Her phone rang from somewhere on the floor, breaking the intimate moment. Paisley groaned, recognizing the ringtone assigned to her assistant at the nonprofit.

"I should get that," she said reluctantly.

Benedict nodded, releasing her.

Paisley padded across the room, retrieving her phone from the pocket of her discarded jeans. "Meredith, hi," she answered, trying to sound as if she hadn't just had the most mind-blowing sex of her life on a kitchen counter.

"Paisley, thank god." Meredith's voice carried an edge of panic. "The Manhattan Mental Health Foundation just moved up the mental health awareness gala."

"What?" Paisley's mind shifted into work mode despite her state of undress. "We don't have the venue secured, the catering—"

"I know, I know." Meredith's typing was audible in the background. "But they're insisting. Something about their board chairman's schedule changing. They're willing to double the donation if we can make it happen."

Paisley caught Benedict watching her, a small smile playing at the corners of his mouth as he observed her transition into professional mode. She held up one finger, silently asking for a moment.

"Double the donation would fund our youth shelter for an entire year," she said to Meredith, mind racing. "Can you call The Plaza? See if their ballroom is available? We had it reserved for next month, but maybe they can accommodate the change. If not, the Meridian Hotel might have availability. "

"Already on it," Meredith confirmed. "But I need you to call the foundation personally. They want to discuss the speaker lineup and press coverage."

"I'll call them within the hour," Paisley promised. "And I'll see if Carson would be willing to serve as the keynote again. Having Crest Strategies' support always brings in more donors."

"Perfect. I'll set that up too." Meredith paused. "Are you okay? You sound... different."

Heat flooded Paisley's cheeks as she caught Benedict's knowing smirk. "I'm fine. Just taking a personal day. Working remotely."

"Oh, good for you! You haven't taken time off in months. Enjoy your 'remote work.'" The air quotes were audible in Meredith's tone. "I'll handle things here."

"Thanks. I'll check in later." Paisley ended the call, turning to face Benedict with a sigh. "Sorry about that."

"Don't apologize." He rose from the couch, the movement drawing her eyes to his still-naked form. "I like watching you work. You're formidable."

"A mental health awareness gala we've been planning for months just got moved up," she explained, running a hand through her tangled hair. "It's going to be a nightmare to reorganize."

"I can help," Benedict offered, walking toward her. "Crest Strategies has connections with every major venue in the city. And if you need a keynote speaker, I'm sure Cars would be happy to step in."

Paisley smiled up at him, touched by the offer. "Thank you. I might take you up on that."

Benedict's hand cupped her cheek, his expression softening. "I'm here for you, Paisley. Not just for the Flintly situation. For everything."

The simple promise made her heart swell. For years, she'd dreamed of having Benedict look at her this way, of being the focus of his fierce protectiveness and loyalty.

"I should probably put on actual clothes," she said reluctantly. "Make those calls about the gala."

"Or," Benedict suggested, his fingers playing with the buttons of the shirt she wore, "we could test out that shower fantasy you mentioned earlier."

Paisley laughed. "I suppose the gala can wait."

Benedict's smile turned predatory as he scooped her into his arms, carrying her toward the master bathroom. "That's what I thought."

LATER, FRESHLY SHOWERED AND DRESSED IN A BORROWED T-shirt and sweatpants that pooled around her feet, Paisley sat cross-legged on Benedict's couch, her laptop balanced on her knees as she coordinated the gala changes. Benedict had retreated to his home office, giving her space to work while he reviewed security footage Penn had sent over.

Her phone buzzed with a text from Meredith.

> Plaza has no availability, but the Meridian Hotel confirmed they do! Working on catering now. Carson's assistant says he'll call you directly about the keynote.

Relief flooded through her. At least something was going right. She texted back her thanks, then set her phone aside, stretching her arms overhead to relieve the tension from hunching over her laptop.

"Good news?" Benedict asked, emerging from his office with a file folder in hand.

"The venue's confirmed for the gala," she explained. "And apparently Carson will be calling me about being the keynote speaker again."

A shadow crossed Benedict's face. "That might be complicated."

"Because of us?" Paisley frowned. "I thought we agreed to keep that separate for now."

"It's not that." He settled beside her on the couch, setting the folder on the coffee table. "Penn found something in the surveillance footage from the park this morning. A second person watching you from the trees on the far side. Not Flintly."

Paisley's stomach dropped. "Someone else from Blackwater?"

"Most likely." Benedict's expression was grim. "Which means they're not just targeting you through Flintly. They have multiple operatives involved."

"Why go to such lengths?" Paisley closed her laptop, setting it aside. "What could they possibly gain from all this?"

"Information is currency in our business," Benedict explained. "If they can prove Crest Strategies engaged in unethical practices, even fabricated evidence, it would destroy our reputation. Our clients would flee to competitors."

"To Blackwater," Paisley concluded.

"Exactly." Benedict's jaw tightened. "This isn't just about revenge for Flintly. It's corporate espionage on a scale I haven't seen before."

This wasn't just about her, or even just about Carson. The entire company, and by extension, every person who worked there, was at risk.

"What can we do?" she asked.

"We fight back." Benedict's voice hardened with determination. "Starting with identifying every Blackwater operative involved."

Before he could elaborate, his phone rang. He glanced at the screen, his expression shifting.

"It's Carson," he said, showing her the display.

Paisley's pulse quickened. "Do you think he suspects something?"

"Only one way to find out." Benedict accepted the call, activating the speaker. "Cars, what's up?"

"I need you in my office." Carson's voice was tense, controlled in a way that made Paisley's stomach clench. "Immediately."

"Problem?" Benedict asked, his own voice perfectly neutral despite the concern in his eyes.

"Not over the phone." A pause. "It's important, Ben. Drop whatever you're doing."

"I'll be there in twenty," Benedict promised.

"Make it fifteen." The call ended abruptly.

Silence fell over the penthouse. Had Carson discovered their relationship somehow? Had something happened with Flintly? With Blackwater?

"You have to go," she said, stating the obvious.

Benedict nodded, already standing. "I don't like leaving you alone."

"I'll be fine here." Paisley rose as well, smoothing hands down the borrowed sweatpants. "Your security system is top-notch, right?"

"The best." He moved to his bedroom, emerging moments later with a sleek black handgun that he checked. "But I'd feel better if you had this."

Paisley stared at the weapon he held out to her. "A gun? Ben, I don't know how to—"

"Safety's here," he explained, demonstrating. "Point and pull the trigger if anyone who isn't me tries to enter. It's registered and legal."

The seriousness in his voice made her take the gun, its weight unfamiliar in her hand. "I really don't think—"

"Please." Benedict's intense gaze met hers. "For my peace of mind."

She nodded, carefully setting the weapon on the coffee table. "Okay. But call me as soon as you know what's going on."

"I will." He cupped her face in his hands, pressing a fierce kiss to her lips. "Lock the door behind me. Don't open it for anyone except me."

"I won't." She leaned into his touch, memorizing the feel of his hands on her skin. "Be careful."

Benedict kissed her once more, lingering as if reluctant to break contact. "I'll be back as soon as I can," he promised.

Paisley watched him gather his jacket and keys, transforming before her eyes back into the controlled, professional Benedict that the world knew. Only his eyes, when they met hers one last time before he left, revealed the man she'd spent the afternoon with. The man who'd confessed twelve years of longing, who'd made love to her with desperate need, who'd held her afterward as if she were precious beyond measure.

The door closed behind him with a definitive click. Paisley engaged the locks as promised, then stood in the empty penthouse, Benedict's borrowed clothes enveloping her in his scent, his gun on the coffee table, his taste still on her lips.

CHAPTER EIGHT

BENEDICT

Benedict entered the Crest Strategies building through the private elevator, straightening his tie as the doors closed behind him. The familiar action helped center his thoughts, pulling him back into the role he'd played for years. Carson's right hand, the surveillance specialist, the controlled professional.

Not the man who'd spent the afternoon fucking Carson's sister.

His body still hummed with the memory of Paisley. Her taste, her scent, the way she'd arched beneath him on his kitchen counter. He forced the images away. Now wasn't the time for distraction, not when Carson's urgent summons suggested something serious had developed.

The elevator doors opened directly into the executive floor. Benedict nodded to the receptionist as he passed, his footsteps silent on the plush carpet as he approached Carson's office. Through the glass walls, his friend and business partner stood hunched over his desk, phone pressed to his ear, free hand raking through his hair.

Whatever this was about, it wasn't good.

Benedict knocked once on the doorframe, and Carson's head snapped up. He ended the call abruptly, gesturing Benedict inside.

"Close the door," Carson instructed, his voice tight.

Benedict complied, scanning his friend's appearance. Carson's normally immaculate suit was rumpled, his tie loosened. Dark circles shadowed his eyes, and a half-empty tumbler of whiskey sat on his desk despite it being barely 5 PM.

"What's going on?" Benedict asked, settling into the chair across from Carson's desk, his posture deliberately relaxed despite the tension coiling in his gut.

Carson sat down and leaned back, running both hands down his face. "Jennings is missing."

Not what Benedict had expected. He kept his expression neutral even as Paisley's warning about her going missing replayed in his mind. How had he forgotten?

"The wife?"

"Yes. Apparently her car was found abandoned with blood stains in the trunk."

"Isn't it just a case of a messy divorce? Shouldn't the police handle it?"

"They should, but Tanner met with Mr. Jennings to discuss business, with my permission, and now it seems someone is trying to make it look like we're involved in Mrs. Jennings disappearance." Carson pushed a file across the desk.

"Is Tanner being questioned?" Benedict asked, opening the file to review the police report. He focused on steadying his breathing, on becoming the analytical strategist they all relied upon.

"He was, but James was with him and basically shut everything down." Carson poured himself another finger of whiskey. "The timing couldn't be worse with everything else going on."

Benedict studied the crime scene photos. "Pays to have a lawyer as a best friend."

"Yeah." Carson leaned forward. "I need you to handle this personally. If someone is trying to make a connection to Tanner's meeting with Jennings, we need to know before the police do."

Flintly's face flashed in Benedict's mind. This had him written all over it.

He should tell Carson about Flintly now. About the Blackwater connection. About everything.

But telling Carson meant explaining how he discovered it, which meant revealing Paisley's involvement. And explaining Paisley's involvement would inevitably lead to questions about why she was staying at his penthouse, why he'd been tracking her movements, why he smelled like her perfume...

"I'll look into it immediately," Benedict said, closing the file. "I'll check our surveillance network, see if we can trace Mrs. Jennings' movements before she disappeared."

Carson nodded, relief evident in the slight relaxation of his shoulders. "Good. And Benedict—"

"Yes?"

"Keep this contained. If word gets out that we're even tangentially connected to a potential homicide, we become a joke."

"I understand." Benedict stood, tucking the file under his arm. "I'll start now. If you want, I'll coordinate with Penn."

"Good." Carson nodded, some of the tension leaving his shoulders. "Let's get out of this mess quickly and quietly. I know you can do it."

The confidence in Carson's voice sent a ripple of discomfort through Benedict. If his friend knew where he'd been just an hour ago —what he'd been doing, and with whom—that confidence would shatter instantly.

"Anything else I should know?" Benedict asked, eager to conclude the meeting before his composure slipped.

Carson hesitated, a shadow crossing his face. "Have you spoken to Paisley recently?"

Benedict's heart rate accelerated, though his external demeanor remained unchanged. "Not in the past few days. Why?"

"I got a call from her nonprofit asking me to be a speaker at some gala. It's sort of the last thing I want to do, considering the circumstances.

"You should do it," Benedict said without hesitation. "I mean, it's a good idea to take attention off potential negative press for the business and instead get some positive word of mouth happening. Don't you think?"

Carson rubbed a hand over his brow. "I guess. I'll make a note to call her about it."

"Good. I'll look into this." He lifted the folder and stepped towards the door. "Call me if you find anything else."

"Of course. Let me know what you find." Carson's attention was already shifting back to his laptop screen.

Benedict exited the office, exhaling slowly once he was out of sight. The meeting had gone better than he'd feared. No suspicion, no confrontation about his whereabouts or relationship with Paisley. Just business as usual, albeit with a missing client and the complication of a potential security breach.

As he made his way toward Penn's office on the floor, Benedict regarded his friends in their offices. Carson wasn't the only one showing signs of stress. James looked haggard as he paced his office, phone pressed to his ear. Tanner was absent, likely handling some crisis that required his particular skill set. Even Penn, visible through the glass walls of his technology suite, appeared more frantic than usual, walking from standing desk to standing desk to type on different computers.

Penn glanced up as Benedict entered. "Carson filled you in on our little problem?"

"The Jennings leak?" Benedict settled against a desk, arms crossed. "Yeah. What have you found?"

"Nothing yet." Penn's attention returned to his screens, where lines of code scrolled faster than most people could read. "But I came back here and started looking into a service breach after you and Paisley came to the Den. If someone's accessing our secure servers, they're good. Really good."

"Better than you?" Benedict raised an eyebrow.

"No one's better than me. Just means I haven't found their entry point yet."

"Could it be physical rather than digital? Someone inside the company?"

"Always possible." Penn's fingers never stopped typing. "But our internal security measures would have flagged unauthorized access to those specific files. And before you ask, yes, I've already checked the logs. Nothing unusual."

Benedict frowned, possibilities multiplying in his mind. "What about client-side vulnerabilities? Like devices brought into the building?"

"Good idea. I'll run a check now." Penn moved to a different computer, typed something in, and then gestured to one of his screens. "Running a remote diagnostics. Should have results in—" He glanced at his watch. "About twenty minutes."

"Good. Keep me updated." Benedict pushed away from the desk. "And have you had a chance to look into Flintly."

Penn's eyes narrowed. "Yeah. The asshole is good. Why?"

"I'm wondering if the security breach has to do with him."

"Definitely could be," Penn murmured, almost to himself.

"Any way to check?"

"Yeah, I sort of already did. And," Penn hesitated, then swiveled in his chair to face Benedict fully. "Remember that program I flagged two months ago? The one that kept trying to probe our firewalls?"

Benedict nodded. They'd discussed it at the time. It had been a sophisticated attempt to access their systems that Penn had ultimately blocked.

"It started again last week." Penn's expression was grim. "Different approach, same digital fingerprint. Someone is very interested in our client files."

"Flintly? Or maybe someone else at Blackwater?" Benedict suggested.

"Possibly." Penn turned back to his screens. "Whoever it is, they're persistent. And getting more sophisticated with each attempt."

"Can we establish a pattern?"

"Already on it." Penn's attention was already absorbed in his work, the conversation effectively over. "I'll let you know when I find something."

Benedict left the technology suite. The timing couldn't be coincidental. Flintly approaching Paisley, digital attacks increasing, information leaking to opponents. It all suggested a coordinated effort to undermine Crest Strategies from multiple angles.

He checked his watch. Nearly six. He'd been gone longer than he'd intended, leaving Paisley alone in his penthouse with only his security system for protection. And a gun. She'd looked absolutely horrified at the idea of using it.

Good thing she probably wouldn't have to.

As the doors closed, Benedict allowed himself a moment of vulnerability no one else would see. He leaned against the wall, closing his eyes briefly. He'd lied to Carson. Hid his relationship with Paisley. Worse, he'd kept the information about Flintly and Blackwater from his best friend despite the fact that it might be the root of all of their problems.

By the time the elevator reached the lobby, Benedict had recomposed himself. He nodded to the security guards as he passed, retrieving his car from the private garage beneath the building. On the drive home, he stopped at Paisley's favorite Italian restaurant, ordering enough food for dinner and breakfast tomorrow. A small gesture, but one he hoped would make her smile.

The thought of returning to her lightened the weight on his shoulders.

Benedict entered his building through the private entrance, bypassing the main lobby. The elevator doors opened directly into his foyer. Benedict disabled the security system, balancing the takeout bags as he moved into the main living area.

"Paisley?" he called, setting the food on the kitchen counter. "I brought dinner."

Silence greeted him, raising the hairs on the back of his neck. The living room lights were on, Paisley's laptop still open on the coffee table, the gun exactly where he'd left it. No signs of struggle or forced entry. The security system had been active when he arrived, which meant no one had entered or exited since he left.

"Paisley?" he called again, moving toward the hallway that led to the bedrooms.

He found her in his home office, standing at the window with her back to the door. After their time together in the shower, he'd taken her to the locked room and explained that he hadn't wanted her going in there before because it held evidence of him watching her. But since they were being honest with each other, and she knew about him keeping an eye on her, there was no reason to keep the office locked. He'd left it open when he'd left for Crest Strategies.

Paisley's posture was rigid, arms wrapped around herself. She didn't turn at his approach, though she must have heard him.

"Hey," he said softly, stopping in the doorway. "Everything okay?"

Paisley turned then, and the expression on her face sent ice through his veins. Her skin was pale, eyes wide.

"He contacted me," she said, her voice surprisingly steady despite her appearance.

Benedict didn't need to ask who. "Flintly."

She nodded, holding out her phone. "Twenty minutes after you left. Somehow he knew we were here together. Knew you'd gone to meet Carson."

Benedict crossed the room in a few swift strides, scanning the message as a fire started to burn inside him. The words were brief.

> Enjoying your time with Astor? Don't get too comfortable. I have something Carson should see. Something about his precious company and the people he trusts. You have a week to get me access to their case files, or I start releasing evidence. And trust me, you don't want that to happen.

Attached were screenshots. They were fabricated but convincing documents showing Carson authorizing illegal surveillance on Theodore Jennings. Financial records with Carson's signature authorizing payments to "eliminate problems." Emails between Carson and Tanner discussing "permanent solutions" to client issues.

All fake. All devastating if released.

"He's targeting the Jennings case specifically," Benedict noted, the connection to Carson's earlier concerns immediately apparent. "That can't be a coincidence."

"There's more." Paisley's voice was hollow as she reached past him to scroll down.

Another attachment appeared. A photograph of them together. It was hard to see through the tinted windows of Benedict's car, but it was definitely taken earlier the first time they'd had sex.

"He's been watching us," she whispered. "All this time."

Benedict's mind raced. "The security breach at the office, the Jennings case and disappearance—it's all connected. All Flintly's work."

"What security breach?" Paisley asked.

"That's part of what Carson wanted to discuss." Benedict straightened, professional instincts overriding emotional responses. "Mrs. Jennings disappearance and a few other instances of someone trying to gain access. But they can't because Penn is too good."

"And now Flintly wants me to give him access to your case files." Paisley ran a hand through her curls. "He wants me to be the leak."

"He's clever. But I think Blackwater is using his vendetta to target our clients."

Paisley wrapped her arms tighter around herself. "What do we do? Now that I know what he's doing, I can't give him access to confidential client information. But if he releases those fabricated documents..."

"He won't." Benedict's voice hardened with certainty. "Because we're going to trap him first."

"How?"

"By giving him exactly what he wants." Benedict moved to his desk. Screens illuminated, displaying security protocols and monitoring software few people knew existed. "Or rather, what he thinks he wants."

Paisley watched him work. "I don't understand."

"We'll provide access to carefully constructed false information," Benedict explained, fingers flying across the keyboard. "Documents that appear legitimate but contain subtle errors. When Blackwater acts on that information, we'll have proof of their corporate espionage."

"Is that even legal?"

The question gave him pause. He looked up at her, realizing how this must appear.

"It's in the gray area," he admitted. "But so is what they're doing to us. Their's is darker grey than ours."

"So we feed him false information. Then what?"

"We track where it goes. See who acts on it?. Build a case against Blackwater that's so airtight they'll never recover. But we'll need help."

"Penn," Paisley concluded.

"Yes. And possibly the others, depending on how this unfolds." Benedict watched her reaction carefully. "That means telling them about us, eventually. About how Flintly approached you initially."

Uncertainty flickered across her features. "And Cars?"

"He'll be pissed, but he'll get over it."

Paisley nodded, then stepped forward, closing the distance between them to rest her head against his chest. Benedict's arms came around her automatically, holding her close.

"So what's our first move?" she asked when they separated, practical once again.

Benedict glanced at the computer screen and her phone next to it, at Flintly's threats and demands. "First, we eat dinner before it gets cold," he said, trying to inject some normality into the situation. "Then we start building our counterstrategy."

"And Penn?" Paisley prompted. "When do we bring him in?"

"Tomorrow." Benedict's arm remained around her waist as he guided her back toward the kitchen. "Tonight is just us. No Flintly, no Blackwater, no complications. Just you, me, some Italian food, and lots of sex."

CHAPTER NINE

PAISLEY

Two weeks since Flintly's demand, and Paisley felt like she was living a double life.

She smoothed the front of her emerald gown, mentally checking off the details of the Manhattan Mental Health Foundation gala. The flowers had arrived on time. The caterers had set up precisely as instructed. The auction items were displayed elegantly in the east wing. On the surface, everything was perfect. A flawless event reflecting her professional competence.

Just like the surface of her life appeared normal while underneath, everything had transformed.

For a week, she'd been slipping carefully crafted information to Flintly through encrypted channels Benedict had established, meeting Flintly's time sensitive demand. She'd been sleeping in Benedict's bed, waking in his arms, building a life intertwined with his while keeping it hidden from everyone who mattered. She'd been lying to her brother every time he called.

Paisley accepted a glass of champagne from a passing server, using the moment to scan the ballroom. The Meridian Hotel glittered with Manhattan's elite, the charity event drawing the wealthy and powerful who wanted their philanthropy photographed and praised. Her gaze found Benedict immediately.

He stood near the bar in a perfectly tailored tuxedo, listening to something James was saying while maintaining his usual posture of alert disinterest. To anyone else, he appeared exactly as he always did. Only Paisley knew that beneath that composed exterior was a man who had whispered her name like a prayer that morning as he moved inside her, his hands gripping her hips with possessive intensity.

Their eyes met briefly across the room, and heat flooded her chest. Two weeks of unleashed passion had done nothing to diminish their hunger for each other. If anything, it had intensified, as if twelve years of denial had created a void that couldn't be filled.

Benedict's expression remained neutral, but she caught the slight darkening of his eyes before he returned his attention to James. Their agreement was clear. Professional distance in public, especially around Carson. The risk of discovery was too great, particularly with Flintly watching their every move.

"There you are."

Paisley turned to find Meredith approaching.

"Everything looks perfect," Meredith said, checking items off her list. "Your brother said he's ready to do the keynote speech in thirty minutes, the silent auction is already exceeding projections, and three board members have commented on how smoothly everything is running."

"Thank you for handling the last-minute changes," Paisley replied, genuinely grateful. The venue switch and accelerated timeline had created logistical nightmares that Meredith had somehow solved.

"That's what you pay me for." Meredith's gaze shifted to something over Paisley's shoulder, her professional demeanor softening. "Isn't that Kinsley Ellis by the entrance? I thought she'd gone into hiding after that scandal."

Paisley turned, spotting her friend instantly. Kinsley stood just inside the ballroom, a vision in red that drew attention despite her obvious discomfort. Paisley's heart ached at the uncertainty in her friend's posture, the vulnerability beneath the polished exterior.

"She's a friend," Paisley explained. "I invited her personally."

"Bold move," Meredith observed. "Half the room is pretending not to stare at her."

"Half the room can go to hell," Paisley replied cheerfully. "I need to check on her. Can you make sure the string quartet starts on schedule?"

Meredith nodded, already moving toward her next task as Paisley made her way to Kinsley. She noticed the way conversations faltered as her friend passed, the mixture of fascination and judgment in the gazes that followed her. Paisley's protective instincts flared. She'd always hated the fickle nature of Manhattan's elite, how quickly they turned on anyone who showed vulnerability or made mistakes.

"Kinsley?" Paisley touched her friend's elbow gently. "I wasn't sure you'd come. How are you surviving?"

Relief flooded Kinsley's features at the sight of a friendly face. "I'm managing. Thanks for the invitation."

"Of course. You know you're always—" Paisley followed Kinsley's gaze to where her brother stood at the bar, watching them with undisguised interest. "Oh. You've spotted my brother. I was actually planning to introduce you two."

"Your brother?"

"Carson Crest. The tall one who looks like he could dismantle someone's entire existence with a single phone call." Paisley couldn't keep the fond exasperation from her voice. "He probably could, actually. Reputation management is his specialty. He's been staring at you since you walked in. I think he sees you as a potential client and is planning to offer you Crest Strategies' services. He has a weakness for helping people rebuild from impossible situations."

As she spoke, Paisley caught Benedict's gaze again from across the room. A slight nod confirmed their plan was still on.

"He would help? What...What kind of help?" Kinsley asked, her attention fixed on Carson.

"Reputation management. Crisis response. He's rebuilt careers from worse wreckage than yours." Paisley allowed herself a mischievous smile, playing the role of supportive friend. "Plus he's single, brilliant, and looks at you like he wants to devour you whole. Could be exactly what you need." She winced dramatically. "As long as you tell me absolutely no details. I have no desire to hear about my brother's sexual exploits."

"You'd be lucky to hear about my exploits," Carson's voice came from behind her, making Paisley jump despite herself.

"Damn it, Cars!" She glared at her brother, her heart racing in her chest. "Jerk."

"Bitch." He grinned at her.

As Paisley watched Carson introduce himself to Kinsley, she felt a twinge of guilt. Her brother had no idea that while he was focused on his newest project, she was planning to sneak off with Benedict to access his office. No idea that for two weeks, she'd been feeding carefully selected information to someone trying to destroy his company. No idea that she was sleeping with his best friend.

"I should let you two talk," Paisley said, glancing between them. "I need to check on the auction items. Carson, be nice to her."

Carson's smile was sharp. "I'm always nice to beautiful women in distress."

Paisley rolled her eyes at her brother's predictable charm before slipping away into the crowd. Rather than heading toward the auction items, she circled back around the perimeter of the ballroom, checking her watch. Twenty minutes before the keynote speech would draw everyone's attention to the stage. Maybe forty-five minutes before the mingling continued and she'd have to make an appearance. Thankfully, with the Plaza pulling out of the event, she didn't have to try to get halfway across town to Crest Strategies. She could simply walk down the street from the hotel. They had factored the timing of everything. Ten minutes to get there and back from the Meridian hotel, twenty minutes to get upstairs to Carson's office, locate the files, and get out before anyone noticed their absence.

She caught Benedict's eye across the room once more. He excused himself from his conversation with James, moving casually toward one of the side exits. Paisley waited thirty seconds before following a different route, her heart rate accelerating with each step.

They had planned the night meticulously over the past week. It was, admittedly, the strangest pillow talk after mind blowing sex that she'd ever had. But they'd covered it all. The timing, the route, the extraction of specific files that would appear valuable to Flintly while containing nothing that could actually damage her brother's company.

She entered Crest Strategies from the side door Benedict had left unlocked earlier that day. The elevator doors opened on the silent executive floor. Just as expected, the lobby to the offices was empty. Paisley stepped out, the soft whisper of her gown against the carpet the only sound in the deserted hallway. Her phone vibrated with a text from Benedict:

> Five minutes behind you. Start on the northeast cabinet.

She made her way to Carson's office. The door opened with a soft click, revealing the familiar space now shrouded in shadows. Paisley flipped on a single desk lamp, careful to keep the illumination minimal.

Paisley moved to the filing cabinet in the northeast corner, using the key Benedict had copied for "emergencies." Inside were client files organized by name, each folder containing strategy documents, contracts, and communications.

Paisley was so focused on her task that she didn't hear the office door open. She startled when strong arms encircled her waist from behind, but the familiar scent of Benedict's cologne instantly calmed her racing heart.

"Right on time," she murmured as his lips brushed her neck.

"Always." His voice was low against her skin. "Did you find everything?"

"Almost." She held up her phone, showing the images she'd captured. "Just a few more pages in the correspondence section."

Benedict reached around her to open another drawer, his body pressed against her back in a way that made concentration increasingly difficult. "These too," he said, extracting a thin folder. "Fake meeting minutes that Penn created yesterday. They look completely authentic, but the dates don't align with our actual strategy sessions."

Paisley nodded, photographing the documents. "Do you think he'll believe it?"

"He'll want to," Benedict replied, his hands still resting on her hips. "People like Flintly see what they expect to see. He's so focused on finding evidence of misconduct that he won't notice the inconsistencies until it's too late."

With the last document photographed, Paisley returned everything to its proper place, careful to leave no trace of their presence. When she turned to face Benedict, he was watching her with an intensity that made her breath catch.

"What?" she asked, suddenly self-conscious.

"You're remarkably good at this," he observed, a hint of admiration in his voice. "The espionage. The deception."

"I don't know whether to be flattered or concerned by that assessment."

Benedict's lips curved into a rare smile. "Both, probably." His hand came up to cup her cheek. "We should get back to the hotel. The keynote will be starting soon."

But he didn't move away. Instead, his thumb traced the curve of her lower lip.

"Ben," she warned, though there was no real resistance in her voice. "We don't have time."

"We have fifteen minutes." His eyes darkened as they dropped to her mouth. "More than enough time for what I'm thinking."

The thrill of danger, of being in Carson's office, of potentially being discovered, heightened every sensation as Benedict's lips found hers. The kiss was hungry, possessive, his hands sliding down her back to pull her closer against him. Paisley melted into him, her arms winding around his neck as she opened to him.

Benedict knew exactly how to touch her, where to apply pressure, when to be gentle and when to demand. His hand slid down to the slit in her gown, finding bare skin beneath.

"I've been thinking about this all night," he murmured against her lips as his fingers traced up her thigh. "You in this damn cocktease of a dress, looking so professional and put-together while only I know what you're really like when you come apart."

Heat pooled low in Paisley's belly. "We really shouldn't," she protested, even as her body arched into his touch.

"We absolutely shouldn't," Benedict agreed, walking her backward until she hit the edge of Carson's desk. "That's what makes it so appealing."

In one fluid motion, he lifted her onto the desk, stepping between her parted thighs. Paisley's head fell back as his mouth found the sensitive spot just below her ear.

"If Carson ever found out," she gasped as Benedict's hand slid higher beneath her dress, bunching it around her waist.

"He won't." Benedict's voice held absolute certainty as he discovered the lace barrier of her underwear. "Unless you're planning to tell him."

"God, no." The thought of her brother's reaction was both terrifying and, in this moment of forbidden intimacy, strangely arousing.

Benedict's fingers slipped beneath the lace, finding her already wet for him. "I should be worried about how good you are at keeping secrets," he murmured, his thumb circling her clit and drawing a gasp from between her lips. "But right now, I'm just grateful."

Paisley stifled a moan as pleasure spiraled through her. The situation was insane. She was spread across her brother's desk while his best friend touched her in ways that would destroy their relationship if ever discovered. And yet she couldn't bring herself to stop, not when Benedict was looking at her like he wanted to devour her, not when her body was responding so eagerly to his touch.

Benedict tore the lace underwear with a sharp tug, the sound of rending fabric filling the quiet office. Paisley gasped, her eyes flying open.

"Hey!" She slapped his shoulder lightly, a laugh bubbling up from her chest. "Those were my favorite pair."

A smirk tugged at the corner of his mouth as he pocketed the ruined lace. "I'll buy you a suitcase full. As long as I get to rip them off you every time."

Heat flushed her cheeks. Before she could respond, Benedict was on his knees, his hands pushing her thighs wider. She leaned back on her elbows, watching him as he dipped his head, his tongue finding her center.

Paisley's head fell back as pleasure shot through her. Benedict licked and sucked, his fingers digging into her thighs, holding her open to his hungry mouth. He growled against her flesh, the vibrations sending shockwaves of sensation coursing through her. When he slid two fingers inside her, she couldn't stifle the shriek and moan that escaped her lips.

"God, you taste incredible," he murmured, his tongue circling her clit before his fingers began to move, curling inside her, stroking that spot that made her see stars.

Her hips bucked against his mouth, her body chasing the release that was building with every lick, every thrust of his fingers. Benedict's free hand slid up her body, sliding the strap of her dress down. He found her breast, exposing it from beneath the fabric. He squeezed, his thumb brushing over her nipple.

The combined sensations sent her spiraling over the edge. Her orgasm crashed through her, her body convulsing as Benedict licked her through it, his fingers slowing but not stopping, drawing out her pleasure until she was a panting, trembling mess.

He stood, helping her to her feet and making sure she was steady. Before she could say anything, though he turned her around, pushing her dress back up to her hips and forcing her hands to brace against the desk.

"We have a little problem, Pai," he whispered. She gasped as his fingers, slick with her arousal, tracing her asshole, pressing gently.

"I don't have a condom," he murmured, his voice low. "And while I know you're taking the pill, I'm not keen to risk a little rug-rat with you yet. Someday. Just not today." He circled her pussy, gathering more moisture before drawing it back up to her ass. Benedict added his saliva to the mixture. "So, I'm going to take you here. And you're going to walk back into that gala with my cum sliding down your thighs."

A shiver of desire racked her body at his words. She pushed back against his fingers, inviting more. He slid one finger in, slowly, letting her adjust to the sensation. Then another, scissoring gently, stretching her.

Paisley gasped, her fingers clutching the edge of Carson's desk as Benedict's fingers pushed deeper. The sensation was foreign, intense, a burning stretch that made her eyes widen and her breath hitch. She'd never... no one had ever taken her in the ass.

"Ben," she breathed, her voice barely more than a whisper. Her body tensed.

"Shh," he soothed, his other hand rubbing her lower back in slow, calming circles. "Relax, Pai. Trust me."

Trust him. She did, implicitly, with every fiber of her being. Taking a deep breath, Paisley forced herself to relax, to lean into the sensation. Benedict's fingers stilled, giving her time to adjust. The burn eased, replaced by a throbbing ache that echoed the pulsing need in her core.

"Good girl," Benedict murmured. He began to move his fingers again, slowly, gently, opening her up. "You're taking my finger so well. So tight. So perfect."

Paisley's cheeks flushed at his words, her body responding to the desire in his voice. She pushed back against his hand, seeking more, her breath coming in short, sharp pants. The sensation was overwhelming, consuming, a dark pleasure that made her heart race and her body ache.

"More," she gasped, her voice barely recognizable. "Ben, please..."

Benedict growled. "That's my fucking girl." He withdrew his fingers, leaving her feeling empty, but before she could protest, fabric rustled followed by the sound of a zipper. Then, the blunt, slick head of his cock was pressing against her, seeking entrance. He spat on his dick, spreading the mixture of saliva and pre-cum around it.

She just hoped it was enough.

Paisley tensed, her body instinctively resisting the intrusion. Benedict's hands gripped her hips, holding her steady. "Relax, Pai," he hummed, his voice strained with the effort of holding back. "Let me in."

Taking a deep breath, Paisley forced herself to relax, to push back against him. The head of his cock breached the tight ring of muscle, and she cried out, her fingers digging into the desk. The burn was intense, consuming, but beneath it was dark, perfect pleasure. Her heart raced and her body trembled.

"That's it," Benedict groaned, his hips flexing as he slowly, carefully, slid deeper. "That's my girl. You're doing so well, Pai. So well." He spit on his cock again, giving it plenty of lubrication.

Paisley's breath hitched, her body stretching to accommodate him. It was too much, too intense, but she wanted it, wanted him. She wanted to feel him inside her, filling her, claiming her in a way no one else ever had.

"Ben," she gasped. "Oh God, Ben...Fuck."

Benedict stilled, his cock buried deep inside her ass. His hands slid up her back, soothing, calming, even as his breath came in ragged gasps. "You okay?" he asked, his voice rough, though it was lined with concern.

Paisley nodded, her fingers relaxing their death grip on the desk. "Yes," she whispered. "Yes, I'm okay." She forced her muscles to relax from where they'd tensed again. "Don't stop."

He began to move, slowly at first, his hips rocking against hers. The sensation was intense, a burn that edged into pleasure as he filled her completely. She could feel every inch of him, the ridge of his head, the veins along his shaft. Fuck, he filled her so completely.

As her body relaxed, accepting him, Benedict's movements grew faster, harder. His hips slammed against hers, driving her against the desk. Her breath came in short gasps, her body alive with sensation. Another orgasm started building, different from the first. More intense.

Benedict's fingers dug into her hips, his body claiming hers with every thrust. The wet sounds of their bodies coming together filled the room, the slap of flesh against flesh. The desk creaked beneath them, the sound of their fucking filling the quiet office.

"Fuck, Pai. You're fucking perfect." He shifted his grip, holding her by the hip with one hand while the other reached between her legs. He stuck two fingers in her pussy, the palm of his hand grinding against her clit.

That's all it took.

In less than two seconds, her orgasm hit her suddenly and her knees nearly gave out. She used the desk to keep herself upright as her body clamped down on Benedict's cock, her cry of pleasure echoing off the walls. Benedict groaned, his body tensing behind her as he found his own release, his cock pulsing inside her, filling her with his hot cum.

"Fuck, baby. That's perfect. You took my dick so well." Benedict pulled out gently, turning her to face him. His eyes were dark, his face flushed with pleasure and exertion. "Are you okay?" he asked again, his fingers brushing a stray curl from her face.

She nodded, a smile tugging at her lips. "Better than okay. That was...wow. Imagine that, but I have a vibrating dildo in my pussy."

He kissed her, his tongue sliding against hers, sharing the taste of their combined pleasure. "We'll do that later tonight."

"I don't actually have a vibrating—"

"I'll make sure there's one by the time we get home."

Home. She liked the sound of that. Benedict stepped back, helping her straighten her gown, his hands lingering on her body as if he couldn't bear to stop touching her.

Paisley glanced at the clock on the wall, her heart skipping a beat. "We need to get back."

Benedict nodded, adjusting his own clothes quickly. He held out a hand to her, a smirk playing at the corner of his mouth. "Ready, Ms. Crest?"

She took his hand. "Of course, Mr. Astor."

CHAPTER TEN

BENEDICT

BENEDICT RARELY ALLOWED DISTRACTIONS WHEN working, but the weight of Paisley settling onto his lap was one he'd grown to welcome over the past month. Her fingers toyed with his tie as she leaned against his chest, her presence softening the sharp edges of his surveillance room.

"You've been staring at these screens for hours," she murmured, pressing a kiss to the underside of his jaw. "Take a break."

"Almost done," he replied, though his arms tightened around her waist, betraying his reluctance to let her go.

Three monitors dominated the wall before them. The first displayed the Crest Strategies lobby, where Carson was escorting Kinsley Ellis through security. Their newest client had become a fixture at the office, her image rehabilitation progressing very well under Carson's personal attention. The fake dating scheme was a bit out of the box for Benedict's best friend, but at least it was working. Kinsley was a sweet girl from the sound of it who had just been caught at a bad time.

"Look at them," Paisley said, nodding toward the screen. "He claims it's all strategic, but I've never seen Carson look at a client like that."

Benedict followed her gaze, noting the way his friend's hand rested at the small of Kinsley's back, the slight tilt of his head as he listened to whatever she was saying.

"You think he's actually falling for her?" Benedict asked, momentarily distracted from his work by the possibility.

"Oh, absolutely." Paisley's certainty was evident in her tone. "He's got that same look you used to get when you thought I wasn't watching. Like he's fighting himself and losing."

Heat crawled up Benedict's neck. The revelation that she'd been watching him too, cataloging his expressions, interpreting his gestures, still caught him off-guard.

"Carson would deny it," he said, turning his attention to the second screen, which displayed the building's perimeter security, recently enhanced after detecting unusual activity last week.

"Of course he would." Paisley's lips returned to his jaw, trailing light kisses that made it increasingly difficult to concentrate on the third screen's complex coding for another Crest Strategies case. "Just like you denied your feelings for me for twelve years."

Benedict's hands slid up her sides, his resolve to finish his work weakening with each press of her lips. The past month had transformed everything. His space, his routines, his carefully maintained boundaries. Paisley had infiltrated every aspect of his life, and he'd let her, surrendering control in ways he'd never imagined possible.

They still hadn't told Carson. The deception weighed on them both, but the timing never seemed right. Carson was preoccupied with Kinsley's image rebuild, with the Jennings cases, with a dozen other high-profile clients that demanded his attention. And beneath those practical excuses lay the uncomfortable truth: neither of them was ready to risk losing him.

The buzzer for Benedict's penthouse interrupted his thoughts. He frowned, checking the security feed on a smaller monitor tucked beneath the main screens.

"It's James," he said, reluctantly shifting Paisley off his lap. "I wasn't expecting him."

"I'll let him in," Paisley offered, straightening her blouse. "You finish whatever you're working on."

Benedict watched her leave the surveillance room, admiring the confident sway of her hips as she moved. A month ago, he would have considered his workspace strictly off-limits to anyone, especially her. Now, he found himself rearranging equipment to make room for the small desk she'd claimed as her own, installing a comfortable couch where she could work while keeping him company.

The sound of voices in the hallway drew his attention back to the present. He closed the case files on the third screen, replacing them with building security footage before James could enter. He and Penn had brought James up to date a few days earlier.

"Sorry to drop by unannounced," James said as Paisley led him into the room. He carried a leather portfolio under one arm, his expression suggesting this wasn't a social call. "Penn found something I thought you should see immediately."

"About Flintly?" Benedict asked.

James nodded, setting the portfolio on the desk and extracting a folder. "Financial records showing significant offshore transfers. Much larger sums than a senior partner at Blackwater should be handling."

Benedict leaned forward, scanning the documents. Bank transfers, shell companies, international accounts.

"He's not just working for Blackwater," Benedict said, the implications crystallizing in his mind.

"No," James confirmed. "Penn thinks he's freelancing for multiple interests. Selling whatever information he can extract from us to the highest bidders."

Paisley moved to stand behind Benedict, her hand resting on his shoulder as she read over it. "So this isn't just about revenge anymore," she observed. "It's business."

"Very profitable business," James added grimly. "And significantly more dangerous for us. Corporate espionage is one thing, selling client secrets internationally is another level entirely."

"Did you tell Carson?" Benedict asked.

"Not yet." James leaned against the desk, his gaze moving between

Benedict and Paisley with a quirked eyebrow. "You're still running point on this, though I'm beginning to question the wisdom of keeping him in the dark."

"It's temporary," Benedict replied. "You know how things work. We take care of our own problems until we need to bring everyone else in."

James studied them both, a hint of amusement breaking through his professional demeanor. "And does that also go for telling him about the two of you?"

Paisley tensed beside him, her fingers tightening on his shoulder. "What do you mean?" she asked, her voice carefully neutral.

"Please." James chuckled. "I've been negotiating high-stakes settlements for fifteen years. I notice when people change their behavior patterns. The only person you're fooling is Carson, and that's because your brother is preoccupied with Ms. Ellis. It's probably for the best right now." He shrugged. "Even Tanner knows," James added when they remained silent. "Though he expressed his awareness through a series of crude hand gestures rather than actual words."

"How long have you known?" Benedict asked.

"Since the gala." James tucked his hands into his pockets. "You're both generally discrete, but there was a decent amount of time where neither of you was in the ballroom. You returned separately, but with the same... disheveled energy."

Benedict suppressed a grimace, but Paisley's laugh broke the tension in the room.

"Well, that's mortifying," she said, though she sounded more amused than embarrassed. Her hand moved to the nape of Benedict's neck, fingers stroking soothingly through his hair. "I told you we weren't as subtle as you thought."

Her touch relaxed him, as it always did. Benedict leaned back in his chair, allowing himself to draw strength from her presence.

"Your secret's safe," James assured them. "But secrets have a way of revealing themselves at the worst possible moments. You should control the narrative while you still can."

"We will," Paisley promised. "Soon. We just need to find the right time."

James nodded. "In the meantime, I suggest we reevaluate our approach with Flintly. If he's selling information to multiple buyers, our controlled leaks might be more dangerous than we anticipated."

Before Benedict could respond, Paisley's phone chimed with an incoming message. She pulled it from her pocket, her expression shifting as she read the screen.

"It's him," she said quietly. "Flintly. He wants to meet."

Benedict was on his feet instantly, moving to read over her shoulder. The message was brief.

> Time for an exchange. Bethesda Fountain, 4 PM. Come alone.

"No," Benedict said immediately. "Too dangerous. We need to cut him off."

"If we stop communicating now, he'll know something's changed," Paisley argued, turning to face him. "We need to maintain the illusion that we're still playing his game."

"I agree with Benedict," James interjected. "Given what we now know about Flintly's activities, sending you to meet him personally represents a stupid risk."

Paisley crossed her arms. "I know how to handle him. And you'll be watching," she added, gesturing to Benedict's surveillance equipment. "If anything seems off, I'll leave immediately."

Benedict's jaw tightened. A month ago, he would have simply forbidden it, would have used his superior knowledge of security protocols to override her objections. Now, he found himself caught between respecting her agency and protecting her safety.

"Paisley—" he began.

"Ben." She stepped closer, her voice softening as she placed her hands on his chest. "I can do this. Trust me. One last meeting, and then we reevaluate our approach based on what James and Penn have discovered."

The appeal in her eyes weakened his resolve. This was the new dynamic between them; partnership rather than protection, collaboration rather than control. It still felt unfamiliar, uncomfortable even, but he was trying.

"I'll leave you two to discuss," James said, gathering his portfolio. "But Benedict, be careful. Flintly is clearly more dangerous than you thought."

After James departed, Benedict pulled Paisley against him, resting his forehead against hers. "I don't like this," he admitted in a low voice.

"I know." She linked her arms around his neck. "But I'll be fine. You'll be watching, and I'll take that panic button you gave me. Nothing will happen in the middle of Central Park in broad daylight."

Benedict wished he shared her certainty. Years of surveillance work had taught him that public spaces often provided the perfect cover for nefarious activities; too many variables, too many potential distractions, too many escape routes.

"Promise me you'll leave at the first sign of trouble," he insisted. "No heroics, no improvisation."

"Promise." She sealed it with a kiss that started gentle but quickly deepened, her body pressing against his with familiar heat.

Benedict allowed himself to be momentarily lost in her. The taste of her lips, the curve of her body against his, the quiet hum of pleasure she made when his hands slid down to her hips. For a moment, there was no Flintly, no danger, no deception. Just Paisley in his arms, safe and warm and his.

Benedict reluctantly broke the kiss, checking his watch. "If we're going to do this, we need to prepare. The meeting's in two hours."

Paisley nodded, stepping back but keeping her fingers linked with his. "I'll change into something less conspicuous. You set up whatever surveillance makes you feel better."

As she left to prepare, Benedict returned to his monitors, pulling up detailed maps of Central Park and security camera placements around the Bethesda Fountain. His instincts screamed that something was wrong.

But he'd promised to trust her judgment. To see her as a partner, not just someone to protect. It was a promise he intended to keep, despite the anxiety coiling in his gut.

Two hours later, Benedict sat in his car near the park entrance, multiple devices monitoring Paisley's movement through the crowded paths. A small screen displayed footage from the button camera he'd insisted she wear, disguised as an innocuous brooch on her jacket. Another tracked her location via the GPS in her phone. A third monitored police band communications in the area.

"I'm approaching the fountain now," Paisley's voice came through the earpiece Benedict wore. "No sign of Flintly yet."

"Stay in the open," Benedict instructed, scanning the button camera feed. "Keep the fountain between you and the treeline to the east."

"Roger that, Commander," she replied, and the smile in her voice evident despite the tension of the situation.

Benedict watched as she positioned herself exactly as he'd suggested, appearing casual to anyone observing.

Ten minutes passed with no sign of Flintly. Benedict's unease grew with each passing moment. Tardiness wasn't typical of Flintly's carefully calculated approach.

"Something's wrong," he said into the microphone.

"I know," Paisley replied quietly. "Should I leave?"

Before Benedict could respond, her phone chimed with an incoming message. He watched through the button camera as she checked the screen, her posture stiffening.

"What is it?" he asked.

"Flintly," she replied, her voice lower now. "He wants me to move to Bow Bridge instead. Says there are too many people at the fountain."

Benedict's blood ran cold. Change of location mid-meeting was a classic extraction tactic. "That's a trap," he said immediately. "Leave the park now. Use the exit to the west."

"He says he knows you're monitoring," Paisley continued, and Benedict could hear the first notes of genuine concern in her voice. "Says if I don't come alone, the deal is off."

"It's not a negotiation, Paisley. Leave now." Benedict was already starting his car, preparing to move closer to her position. "Something is very wrong."

To his relief, he saw her begin moving toward the western exit as instructed. "I'm leaving," she confirmed. "Meeting you at the car."

Benedict watched her progress on the GPS tracker, his tension easing as she moved away from the fountain. Then his phone buzzed with a message from an unknown number:

> You've been feeding me false information, Astor. Time to raise the stakes.

Attached was a photo taken seconds ago—Paisley walking along a park path, a man in a dark jacket following at a discreet distance.

"Pai, you're being followed," he said urgently into the microphone. "Man in a dark jacket, about twenty yards behind you. Do not confront. Continue to the exit, but be ready to run if necessary."

"I see him," she replied, her voice steady. "There's another one ahead, near the hot dog stand."

Benedict cursed under his breath. Two operatives meant a coordinated effort, not just surveillance but potentially an interception.

"Change your course," he instructed, already pulling away from his parking spot. "Head north toward the 72nd Street exit. I'll meet you there."

"On my way," she confirmed.

Benedict watched her location tracker change direction, moving north as instructed. The button camera showed a crowded pathway ahead—tourists, joggers, families with strollers. Good. Witnesses would make an abduction more difficult.

His phone buzzed again:

> Call off your tracking dogs, Astor. This is between Paisley and me now.

Followed by another message.

> Too late. Should have been honest from the beginning.

Benedict's heart rate spiked. The GPS tracker showed Paisley still moving steadily north, but something felt wrong. He tried the earpiece.

"Paisley, report." No response. "Pai, can you hear me?"

Nothing but static.

Benedict floored the accelerator, weaving through traffic toward the park's northern entrance. The GPS tracker still showed movement, but the button camera had gone dark. Had it been discovered? Disabled?

Traffic crawled along Central Park West, each minute stretching Benedict's nerves tighter. He abandoned his car three blocks from the park, continuing on foot at a sprint. His phone buzzed with another message from Flintly.

> Come on now, Astor. How much is she really worth to you?

Benedict burst into the park, racing toward the location indicated on the GPS tracker. The pathway was crowded with afternoon visitors, none of whom matched Paisley's description. He pushed forward, scanning faces.

He reached the spot where Paisley's tracker indicated she should be. Nothing. Just an empty bench overlooking a small pond. Then he saw her phone placed deliberately in the center of the bench.

Cold dread washed over him as he picked it up. The screen lit up with a text notification:

> If you want to see her again, bring the complete unredacted Jennings divorce files to the storage facility at 133 West End Avenue, Unit 27. You have two hours. The REAL files, Astor, not your sanitized versions. Come alone or she dies.

Attached was a photo that made Benedict's blood freeze in his veins. Paisley, unconscious, bound with zip ties in what appeared to be the trunk of a car. A dark bruise was forming along her temple where she'd clearly been struck.

Benedict's mind raced through options. The unredacted Jennings files contained damaging information about Carson's methods—not illegal, but certainly ethically questionable. Information that, if released publicly, could destroy Carson's reputation and potentially Crest Strategies itself.

Information that would give Flintly exactly what he needed to sell to his highest bidders.

His first instinct was to call for backup; to mobilize Tanner's contacts, Penn's technical expertise, James's legal connections. Together, they could locate the storage facility, create a plan, extract Paisley safely.

But Flintly's warning was explicit: come alone, or Paisley dies.

His phone rang with an incoming call from Carson. Benedict stared at the screen, the name of his best friend—the man whose sister he loved, whose trust he'd betrayed—flashing insistently.

Benedict declined the call, making his decision. He would handle this alone. Would face whatever Flintly had planned. Would bring the files that could potentially destroy everything he and Carson had built.

Because none of it mattered if Paisley wasn't safe.

As he raced toward the Crest Strategies office to retrieve the Jennings files, Benedict's mind raced. He should have trusted his instincts. Should have insisted on accompanying her. Should have recognized the trap before it was sprung.

His phone buzzed with another message from Flintly:

90 minutes remaining. Tick tock.

Attached was another photo of Paisley, now conscious, her eyes blazing with fury despite the gag in her mouth. He couldn't make out the background completely. It looked like metal though. Despite nothing to help him figure out where he'd taken her, the message was clear: she was alive, but her condition could change at any moment.

For twelve years, he'd protected Paisley from a distance, watching over her, keeping her safe from threats she never knew existed. Now she was in danger precisely because of her connection to him. Because he'd allowed his personal feelings to override his judgment.

Because he'd tried to have everything—her love, Carson's trust, his career—instead of making the difficult choice that might have kept her safe.

As he reached the Crest Strategies building, Benedict felt like he had a bomb strapped to his chest. The files he was about to steal would destroy Carson's career if released publicly. The brother of the woman he loved would be ruined by Benedict's own hand.

But the alternative was unthinkable.

Benedict swiped his security card at the private entrance, bypassing the main lobby where he might be seen. As the elevator carried him toward the executive floor, he made a silent promise:

He would get Paisley back. And then he would destroy Dawson Flintly, no matter the cost.

CHAPTER ELEVEN

PAISLEY

PAIN THROBBED THROUGH PAISLEY'S TEMPLE, DRAGGING her back to consciousness. The surface beneath her was cold and hard. Metal, her foggy brain eventually registered. She kept her eyes closed, fighting the urge to groan as she assessed her situation.

Her head pounded where she'd been struck. Shoulders ached from being wrenched behind her, though she wasn't currently restrained. No zip ties. No rope. Small mercies.

Her memories returned in fragments: Central Park. Flintly's text. The man following her. Trying to reach the exit. Then nothing. A blank space where consciousness should have been.

Paisley slowly opened her eyes, blinking against the dim light filtering through small ventilation slats near the ceiling. A shipping container. She was inside what appeared to be a standard cargo unit, the kind loaded onto freight ships and semi-trucks. The space was mostly empty except for a few wooden pallets stacked against one wall.

She pushed herself to sitting position, wincing at the wave of dizziness that followed. Concussion, probably. The metallic taste of blood lingered in her mouth where she'd bitten her cheek.

"Hello?" she called, then immediately regretted it. The sound reverberated painfully inside her skull, and the echo confirmed what she already suspected. She was alone in a sealed metal box. No one would hear her. No one who could help, anyway.

Paisley took stock of her situation. The container measured roughly forty feet long by eight feet wide. The only exit was a set of double doors at one end, secured from the outside. The ventilation slats provided minimal air circulation and the faintest hint of light, but they were too small for escape and positioned too high to reach.

Her jacket, shoes, and phone were gone. She still wore her jeans and blouse, though the latter was torn at the sleeve. Her brooch camera had been discovered and removed. The lipstick panic button was gone too.

No visible surveillance equipment inside the container, but that didn't mean she wasn't being watched. Flintly had proven sophisticated in his intelligence gathering.

Flintly. Dawson Flintly. The man she'd been manipulating for weeks while he'd apparently been doing the same to her. She'd known he was dangerous, but this level of escalation suggested something had changed. Something had pushed him over the edge from corporate espionage to violent abduction.

The false information. Benedict had been right. Feeding Flintly carefully doctored files had been too risky. He must have discovered their deception.

Paisley leaned against the metal wall, closing her eyes against another wave of pain. What was Benedict doing now? She could picture him all too clearly. He would be hunting for her. Would he call Carson? Would he involve the team? Or would his protective instincts drive him to handle this alone?

A selfish part of her hoped he would call Carson, would bring the full resources of Crest Strategies to find her. But the part that knew Benedict, truly knew him, beyond the mask he showed the world, understood he would try to protect her himself. Would see her abduction as his personal failure, his responsibility to correct.

Would possibly walk into a trap to save her.

The thought sent a chill through her that had nothing to do with the metal container's cool temperature.

Paisley forced herself to stand, ignoring the dizziness that threatened to topple her. She needed to think. Needed to find a way out, or at least a way to defend herself when whoever locked her in here eventually returned.

If they returned.

She examined the container more carefully, running her hands along the seams of the walls, looking for structural weaknesses. Nothing. The cargo unit was solid steel, designed to withstand ocean crossings and rough handling. The ventilation slats were the only potential vulnerability, but they were too small and too high.

Turning her attention to the pallets, she examined them for anything useful. The wood was splintered in places. If she could break off a piece, she might have something approaching a weapon. Not much against a gun, but better than nothing.

As she worked at loosening a jagged slat of wood, Paisley's thoughts returned to Benedict. To Carson. To the web of lies and tattered secrets that had led to this moment.

For a month, she'd been living a double life. Feeding carefully selected information to Flintly while falling deeper in love with Benedict. Playing the supportive sister to Carson while lying to his face every time they met. All justified by the greater good, by the need to protect Crest Strategies from an external threat.

And now here she was, trapped in a shipping container with a concussion and a splinter of wood for protection, waiting for her captor to return.

The wood finally broke free with a crack that echoed in the confined space. Paisley examined her makeshift weapon, about fifteen inches long, with a jagged end that could do damage if applied with enough force to vulnerable areas. Eyes. Throat. Groin.

She tucked the wooden shard into the waistband of her jeans at the small of her back, covering it with the loose fabric of her blouse. Positioning herself near the wall adjacent to the doors, she waited where she would be partially hidden when they opened.

Minutes or hours passed. Time was difficult to track in the dimly lit container. Paisley struggled to stay alert, fighting the concussion's effects. She ran through scenarios in her mind, planning responses for whatever might come next.

Eventually, the sound of approaching footsteps broke the silence. Paisley tensed, her hand moving to the wooden shard at her back. Keys jangled, metal scraped against metal as a padlock was removed. The double doors creaked open, allowing harsher light to spill into the container.

Paisley squinted against the sudden brightness, trying to make out the figure silhouetted in the doorway. She recognized Flintly immediately; average height, unremarkable features, the blandness that had allowed him to operate undetected for so long. What she hadn't seen in their previous meetings was the gun held comfortably in his right hand.

"Good, you're awake." His voice carried the same pleasant, unthreatening tone he'd used in their meetings. "Step away from the wall, Ms. Crest. Hands where I can see them."

Paisley hesitated, calculating her odds. The wooden shard suddenly seemed laughably inadequate against the semi-automatic pistol pointed casually in her direction.

"Now, please." Flintly's tone remained conversational, but something in his eyes had changed. The mask of the concerned informant had slipped, revealing something colder beneath. "I'd rather not shoot you just yet. That would disrupt the timeline."

Timeline. The word sent a fresh wave of dread through her. Whatever Flintly had planned, it was methodical. Structured. Not a heat-of-the-moment kidnapping but something calculated.

Paisley stepped forward slowly, hands raised to shoulder height, leaving the wooden shard hidden at her back. "What timeline would that be, Dawson?" she asked, deliberately using his real name. "Or do you prefer I keep calling you Marcus?"

A flicker of surprise crossed his features, quickly replaced by a smile that didn't reach his eyes. "I see Astor has been doing his homework. Good for him."

"He knows everything about you," Paisley bluffed, watching for a reaction. "Your connection to Blackwater. Your side deals with other buyers. The team is tracking your movements as we speak."

Flintly chuckled, the sound devoid of humor. "If that were true, they'd be here already." He gestured with the gun. "Sit down. Center of the container, please. We're going to have a conversation."

Paisley complied, settling cross-legged on the metal floor, careful to keep the wooden shard concealed. Flintly remained standing in the doorway, positioning himself so the light remained at his back, keeping his face partially shadowed while illuminating hers.

"What do you want?" she asked directly. "If it's information, this seems like an extreme approach."

"Information is merely a commodity," Flintly replied. "One I've been trading quite profitably. But this—" he gestured between them with the gun, "—this is about something more personal."

"Revenge," Paisley concluded. "Because Benedict caught you selling client information."

Flintly's expression hardened slightly. "Astor didn't just catch me. He destroyed me. Tried to make sure I couldn't work anywhere in reputation management again. Took everything I'd built and burned it to the ground."

"And now you're doing the same to him."

"No." Flintly's smile returned, colder now. "What I'm doing is much more elegant. Blackwater will acquire what remains of Crest Strategies after the scandal breaks. A corporate takeover facilitated by tragedy."

"You mean Mrs. Jennings?"

"No," Flintly chuckled. "No, her husband is the one who killed her. It's just too easy to shift it onto your brother. No, I'm talking about a different tragedy."

The clinical way he spoke sent ice through Paisley's veins. "What tragedy?"

"The murder-suicide, of course." Flintly leaned against the door-frame, as casual as if discussing the weather. "Carson Crest, driven to desperation when his sister threatened to expose his unethical business practices. Tragically kills her to silence her, then takes his own life when the truth begins to emerge anyway."

Horror washed over Paisley. "You're going to kill me and frame Carson."

"Eventually." Flintly nodded. "But not quite yet. First, we need Benedict to deliver the unredacted Jennings files, the ones that prove Carson authorized illegal surveillance, witness intimidation, all the unsavory methods Crest Strategies employs when necessary."

"Those files don't exist," Paisley countered. "Because those things didn't happen."

Flintly's laugh was genuine this time. "You really don't know, do you? Your brother, your lover—they've kept you in the dark about the real nature of their business. Crest Strategies doesn't just manage reputations, Ms. Crest. They manufacture them. They destroy people who get in their way. They bury evidence. They create false narratives."

"You're lying," Paisley said, but doubt crept into her voice. Something Benedict had said weeks ago, came back to the forefront of her mind. Blackwater used unethical means while her brother and the guys at Crest Strategies used ethical ones on *most* cases.

He'd said most.

"Am I?" Flintly raised an eyebrow. "Ask yourself why Benedict never fully explained his surveillance operations to you. Why certain clients meet only with Carson, never the full team. Why Penn Levine keeps company technological security so locked down. Why Tanner Whitney, with his particular skill set, is considered essential to Crest Strategies' success. Why they need that fucking lawyer, James Rothschild, on the team."

Paisley maintained her composure despite the growing unease in her stomach. "If you hate them so much, why work for their competitor? Why not leave the industry entirely?"

"Because justice requires proximity." Flintly's expression darkened. "And because Blackwater recognizes talent, regardless of past affiliations. They understood the value of my inside knowledge of Crest's operations."

"So this is all for a promotion?" Paisley couldn't keep the disgust from her voice. "You're kidnapping me, planning multiple murders, for a better position at Blackwater?"

"Among other compensations." Flintly checked his watch. "Your boyfriend should be gathering the files I requested by now. Once he delivers them, I'll have everything I need to complete the narrative. The evidence of Carson's unethical practices and the motive for silencing his whistleblower sister. It'll be a wonderfully tragic conclusion to the Crest family saga."

"And Benedict?" Paisley asked, though she feared she already knew the answer.

"Will join you. Found dead at the scene, implicated in helping Carson cover up his crimes before a crisis of conscience led him to attempt to save you. Too late, of course."

"You won't get away with this," Paisley said, the cliché slipping out before she could stop it.

"I already have." Flintly straightened, adjusting his grip on the gun. "The pieces are in motion. Benedict will bring the files because he believes it will save you. Carson will be implicated because the evidence will be irrefutable. And you—" he gestured with the gun, "—will be the tragic victim whose death exposes it all."

Paisley's mind raced, looking for weaknesses in his plan, for anything she could use. "You've overlooked something," she said, stalling for time. "James, Penn, Tanner—they'll know the truth. They'll expose you."

"Without evidence? Without witnesses?" Flintly shook his head. "They'll be too busy trying to salvage what's left of their reputations after Crest Strategies implodes. Besides, they're not my concern. My arrangement with Blackwater covers only Carson and Benedict."

"Arrangement," Paisley repeated. "Blackwater authorized this? They know what you're planning?"

Flintly hesitated only for a second. "Blackwater understands the need for decisive action in corporate acquisitions. The specifics are left to my discretion."

A crack in his composure. Paisley seized it. "They don't know. This isn't a sanctioned operation. It's your personal vendetta. If Blackwater knew you were planning multiple murders, they'd cut ties immediately."

"Enough." Flintly's pleasant mask slipped completely, his face hardening. "It doesn't matter what Blackwater knows or doesn't know. The plan proceeds regardless."

Paisley saw her opening. She shifted, preparing to lunge for the gun. "And what about your family? Your friends? Do they know you're planning to become a murderer? Or have you isolated yourself so completely that no one would even notice if you disappeared?"

Rage flashed across Flintly's face. "You know nothing about me—"

Paisley launched herself forward, covering the distance between them. Her hand closed around his wrist, forcing the gun upward as her other hand scrambled for the wooden shard at her back. Flintly reacted, his free hand clamping around her throat as he slammed her against the metal wall of the container.

The impact jarred the wooden shard from her grasp. It clattered to the floor as Paisley struggled for breath, her fingers clawing at Flintly's hand around her throat.

"Predictable," he hissed, his face inches from hers. "Benedict taught you well, but not well enough."

He reversed the gun in a smooth motion, bringing the butt of it crashing against her temple, the same spot where she'd been struck earlier. Pain exploded through Paisley's skull, her vision swimming with darkness. She slid down the wall as Flintly released her, gasping for breath as her knees hit the metal floor.

"That was foolish," Flintly said, his voice returning to its earlier conversational tone. "But educational. I'll need to take additional precautions when your boyfriend arrives."

Paisley forced herself to look up, fighting against the darkness threatening to consume her vision. "He'll kill you," she managed, each word an effort. "When he finds out what you've done, what you're planning, Benedict won't stop until you're dead."

Flintly crouched before her, tilting his head as if studying a curious specimen. "That's what I'm counting on," he said softly. "His emotional response. His desperation to save you. It's what will make him careless. Make him vulnerable."

He straightened, adjusting his jacket. "Rest while you can, Ms. Crest. The next few hours will be quite demanding for both of us."

Flintly backed out of the container, never turning his back to her. The heavy doors swung shut, plunging Paisley back into dim half-light. The padlock clicked into place, sealing her in once more.

Alone in the darkness, Paisley allowed herself one moment of pure, undiluted fear. A sob escaped her throat, echoing hollowly in the metal box. Pain radiated from her temple where she'd been struck twice now. Her neck throbbed where Flintly's fingers had dug into her flesh.

But beneath the pain and fear, something else burned. Rage. At Flintly for his calculated cruelty. At herself for underestimating him. At the universe for taking something as beautiful as her newfound love with Benedict and twisting it into a weapon against them both.

Paisley forced herself to breathe deeply, to push past the pain and focus. She wasn't dead yet. Which meant there was still a chance. Still hope.

She crawled to where the wooden shard had fallen, retrieving it from the shadows. A poor weapon, but the only one she had. She examined the area around the doors more carefully, looking for structural weaknesses, for anything she might have missed in her earlier assessment.

The hinges. From the inside, she could see the bottom pin of one hinge was slightly rusted, the metal corroded from exposure to the elements. It wasn't much, but with enough force applied at the right angle, she might be able to compromise it.

As she worked the wooden shard into the small gap between the hinge and the door, Paisley thought of Benedict. Of his brilliant mind, his careful planning, his ability to see three steps ahead in any situation. What would he do in her position?

He would analyze the enemy's plan, looking for logical flaws. And Flintly's plan, for all its calculated cruelty, had one significant weakness: it required Benedict to deliver the files personally. To walk into a trap he would almost certainly recognize.

Benedict wouldn't come unprepared. Wouldn't come without a contingency plan. Wouldn't sacrifice himself without ensuring her safety first.

The knowledge gave her strength as she worked at the rusted hinge, ignoring the fresh pain in her head and the growing darkness at the edges of her vision. Benedict was coming. And whatever Flintly thought he knew about the man she loved, Paisley knew him better.

CHAPTER TWELVE

BENEDICT

Benedict moved through the Crest Strategies offices, his face a mask of professional detachment that betrayed nothing of the storm raging inside him. His footsteps blended with the ambient sounds of the workday as he made his way toward Carson's office where the unredacted Jennings files were stored.

Seventy-eight minutes until Flintly's deadline.

He nodded casually to Carson's assistant, who was gathering her things for a coffee run. "Carson in?" he asked.

"No, he's with Ms. Ellis," she replied. "Need me to call him?"

"No need," Benedict assured her with a practiced smile. "Just dropping off some files. I'll let myself in."

She nodded. Benedict waited until she disappeared around the corner before entering Carson's office, closing the door silently behind him.

The corner office was immaculate as always. Benedict moved to the locked cabinet and used his spare key.

It didn't take him long to find the case file. The unredacted documents contained everything Flintly had demanded. Carson's authorization for enhanced surveillance, James's aggressive legal maneuvers, detailed intelligence on Theodore Jennings's vulnerabilities through Tanner. Nothing illegal, but certainly ethically questionable.

Benedict's fingers hesitated, the weight of twelve years of friendship crushing his chest. Every principle he'd built his career on, loyalty, discretion, trust, crumbled beneath the single, overwhelming need to keep Paisley safe.

"I'm sorry, Carson," he whispered to the empty office. "I know you'd do the same thing for her, but... I'm sorry."

Carson had stood beside him through everything. The founding of Crest Strategies, the lean years, the triumphs. They'd sworn to protect each other's interests above all else. Now Benedict was violating that trust, stealing the very information they'd both sworn to safeguard.

Images flashed through his mind: Carson's hand on his shoulder after their first major client signing; the fierce loyalty in his friend's eyes when competitors tried to poach Benedict; the unconditional trust when Carson had handed him access to everything they'd built.

And Paisley. Her face in that photo Flintly had sent, the terror in her eyes, the bruise forming on her temple.

Benedict's jaw clenched so hard he tasted blood. This choice—between the man who'd been his brother in everything but blood and the woman he'd silently loved for over a decade—tore at him. But there was no real choice. Not really. Not when it came to Paisley's life.

"You would do the same," Benedict told himself. "I'll make this right," he promised the ghost of his friendship. "Somehow. I'll get her back. You'll understand. You have to."

As he transferred the documents to his secure briefcase, Benedict pulled out his personal laptop, establishing a separate connection. He began creating duplicates of the files, but with subtle modifications; metadata that would allow Penn to track them if they were uploaded to servers, digital markers that would identify any distribution channels. A breadcrumb trail that would lead back to whoever received these files from Flintly.

"Little late for spring cleaning."

Benedict didn't startle at the unexpected voice, though his hand moved instinctively toward the gun concealed beneath his jacket. He turned to find Tanner filling the doorway, massive arms crossed over his chest, expression blank as usual.

"Working," Benedict replied, not pausing in his task.

Tanner stepped into the office, closing the door behind him. He moved with surprising grace for a man his size, coming to stand beside Benedict. His gaze tracked the file names displayed on the laptop screen.

"Jennings files." Tanner's voice was a low rumble. "Unredacted."

It wasn't a question, but Benedict nodded anyway. "I need them."

"For?"

"Can't tell you."

Tanner shifted, positioning himself between Benedict and the door. "Try again."

The file duplication completed with a soft chime. Benedict closed his laptop, securing it in his briefcase alongside the original documents.

"I don't have time for this," he said, moving to step around Tanner.

Tanner didn't budge. "Make time."

Benedict met the larger man's gaze directly, weighing his options. Tanner Whitney had been recruited early on specifically for his unique skill set, a combination of military training, tactical expertise, and absolute loyalty. He spoke rarely but observed constantly. And right now, he'd clearly observed enough to know something was wrong.

"Paisley's been taken," Benedict said finally, forcing his voice to stay neutral.

Tanner's expression didn't change, but a muscle in his jaw tightened. "When?"

"Less than an hour ago. Central Park."

"By?"

"Dawson Flintly."

Understanding flickered in Tanner's eyes. "The asshole from a few years ago."

Benedict nodded. "He's demanding these files in exchange for her release."

"And you're going alone." Again, not a question.

"He was explicit. No team. No authorities."

Tanner's gaze dropped to the briefcase where Benedict had stashed the files. "You'll give him everything?"

"I'll give him what I need to," Benedict replied. "She's more important."

A ghost of a smile touched Tanner's lips. "Doctored copies?"

"With tracking elements."

"Good." Tanner stepped aside, clearing the path to the door. "Where's the exchange?"

"Storage facility on West End. I need to go. Alone."

"Bullshit. I'm coming."

"Tanner—"

"Nope. You need backup. Don't be a fucking idiot."

Benedict weighed his options. Having Tanner involved complicated things, introduced variables he couldn't control. But it also improved their chances of extracting Paisley safely. Of ending Flintly's threat permanently.

"He'll be watching the approach," Benedict said, relenting. "You'll need to remain unseen."

Tanner snorted. "My specialty."

"And Carson can't know. Not yet."

"About the files? Or about you fucking his sister?"

Benedict's composure slipped for a fraction of a second before he regained control. "Both."

Tanner studied him for a long moment. Then he gave a single, sharp nod. "Your secret. Your call."

It was as close to approval as Tanner ever offered.

"Okay. We need to move," Benedict said, checking his watch. "Sixty-three minutes to deadline."

"My truck's downstairs." Tanner was already heading for the door. "Extra gear in the back."

Benedict followed, his mind recalibrating to accommodate the new development. Having Tanner involved was both a risk and an advantage. The man was a walking arsenal, with contacts throughout the city's shadowy underbelly. If anyone could provide effective backup while remaining invisible, it was Tanner Whitney. Well, him and their security expert, Jenna Briggs. But she was busy elsewhere, it seemed. Probably for the best. She was a bit more tight-laced than the mountain of a man next to him.

They rode the elevator in silence. As they crossed the parking garage toward Tanner's massive black pickup, Benedict allowed himself a moment of brutal honesty.

He'd been wrong to handle this alone. Wrong to keep Paisley's abduction from the team. Wrong to believe he could control every variable, anticipate every threat. The very qualities that made him effective at his job—his methodical planning, his obsessive attention to detail, his need for control—had blinded him to the most obvious solution: trust his team.

Trust others.

Something he'd struggled with his entire life, and especially since meeting Paisley. The irony wasn't lost on him—the surveillance expert who observed everything had failed to see his own critical weakness.

"You good?" Tanner asked as they reached the truck.

"Fine," Benedict replied automatically.

Tanner gave him a look that clearly communicated his disbelief. "She's a tough son of a bitch. Fucking smart too. She'll survive us all."

Benedict nodded, unable to voice his gratitude without risking his composure.

Inside the truck, Tanner handed Benedict a small metal case. "Comms. Military-grade. Untraceable."

Benedict opened it to find two earpieces with throat microphones; equipment far beyond commercial availability. He raised an eyebrow at Tanner, who shrugged.

"Insurance policy."

Benedict didn't ask where Tanner had acquired military-grade communications equipment. Some questions were better left unasked. He fitted the earpiece, adjusting the throat microphone to sit comfortably against his skin.

"Range?" he asked, testing the connection.

"Half-mile, clear transmission." Tanner pulled out of the parking garage, the powerful truck accelerating smoothly into traffic. "Two miles with interference."

"Encrypted?"

"Triple."

Benedict nodded, satisfied. "I'll approach from the front. You take a position at the south entrance."

"Done." Tanner navigated through late-afternoon traffic with surprising dexterity for a larger vehicle size. "Extraction plan?"

"Once I confirm Paisley's location, I'll signal. We move simultaneously. You secure the exits, and get her out if I can't."

"And Flintly?"

"He's mine."

Tanner's expression didn't change, but something like approval flickered in his eyes. He nodded once. Flintly had crossed a line. There would be consequences.

The rest of the drive passed in tactical discussion—approach vectors, contingency plans, signals. Benedict's mind settled into the familiar patterns of operational planning, the chaos of emotion temporarily subsumed by the clarity of purpose. This was what he excelled at: anticipating threats, neutralizing variables, controlling outcomes.

But beneath the false calm, fear gnawed at him. Fear that they would be too late, that Flintly would harm Paisley to spite him, that his actions had already set in motion a sequence of events he couldn't stop.

Fear that even if they rescued her physically, she might never forgive him for putting her in danger. For believing he could protect her without trusting her.

Fear that she was already dead.

As they approached the storage facility, Tanner pulled into an alley two blocks away, killing the engine.

"Forty-one minutes," he noted, checking his watch.

Benedict nodded, retrieving the briefcase with the modified files. "I'll approach on foot. Give me five minutes, then move into position."

Tanner reached behind the seat, producing a sleek black case. He opened it to reveal an assortment of weapons and tactical gear. "Take what you need."

Benedict selected a secondary handgun, smaller than his own but equally lethal, securing it in an ankle holster. He added a tactical knife and a small device that—Tanner explained—would temporarily disable electronic locks.

"Extraction signal?" Tanner asked, arming himself.

Benedict tapped his ear. "Three clicks, pause, two clicks."

Tanner nodded. "Trouble signal?"

"Continuous click for three seconds."

"If I don't hear either within twenty minutes of you entering, I'm coming in."

Benedict knew better than to argue. He checked his watch one final time. "Thirty-eight minutes. Let's move."

The late afternoon sun cast long shadows as he exited the truck, the city sounds still vibrant in the industrial area. Benedict moved with long strides, his senses hyperalert. To any observer, he would appear as nothing more than a businessman on a late-day errand. His suit was immaculate, his posture confident, his expression neutral.

Only someone who knew him well would notice the deadly focus in his eyes, the slight tension in his shoulders, the way his hand remained close to his concealed weapon.

The storage facility loomed ahead, a sprawling complex of identical units separated by chain-link fencing. Security cameras dotted the perimeter, their red lights blinking steadily in the golden afternoon light. Benedict noted their positions, calculating blind spots and coverage angles.

Unit 27 was located near the center of the complex, accessed via a main gate that would undoubtedly be watched. Benedict circled the perimeter once, confirming what he'd suspected; Flintly had chosen the location carefully, positioning himself with clear sightlines to all approaches.

But even the most careful planners made mistakes. The cameras had standardized sweep patterns, creating predictable windows of opportunity. The fence had been repaired in sections, leaving one panel slightly lower than the others. The security guard at the main entrance checked his phone every four minutes, creating a consistent distraction.

Small vulnerabilities that, combined, created an opening.

Benedict timed his approach to coincide with the guard's phone check, slipping through the main gate while the man's attention was diverted. He moved through the complex as if he belonged there, using the storage units themselves as cover from the security cameras.

Unit 27 came into view, identical to its neighbors except for the padlock securing its rolling door. Benedict scanned the surrounding area, noting a black sedan parked nearby. Flintly's vehicle, most likely. The windows were tinted, making it impossible to determine if anyone was inside.

"In position," Tanner's voice murmured through the earpiece. "South entrance secured. No movement."

"Approaching target," Benedict replied softly. "One vehicle visible. No visual on subject."

He checked his watch. Thirty-two minutes until Flintly's deadline. Arriving early was a risk. It might catch Flintly off-guard, disrupt whatever preparations he'd made. Or it might trigger contingency plans Benedict hadn't anticipated.

Either way, he couldn't wait any longer. Not with Paisley's life at stake.

Benedict approached Unit 27 directly, making no attempt to conceal his presence. If Flintly was watching, as he almost certainly was, Benedict wanted him to see a man who believed he had no choice but to comply. A man desperate enough to surrender valuable information for someone he loved.

The latter, at least, was not a pretense.

He stopped before the unit's rolling door, standing in the pool of light cast by the overhead security lamp. Exposed. Vulnerable. Exactly as Flintly would want him.

"Show yourself. I know you're watching me," Benedict said, his voice carrying in the relative quiet. "I have what you asked for."

For a moment, nothing happened. Then the black sedan's driver's door opened and Flintly emerged. He looked similar to the way Benedict remembered from years ago—average height, unremarkable features, the blandness that had allowed him to operate undetected within Crest Strategies for so long before Benedict had caught him.

He held a gun in his hand, and in his eyes was a coldness that had replaced the desperate anger of their last encounter.

"Astor." Flintly's voice carried the same pleasant, unthreatening tone Benedict remembered. "Right on time. Always so punctual."

"Where is she?" Benedict asked, ignoring the pleasantries.

Flintly smiled, the expression not reaching his eyes. "Safe. For now." He gestured with the gun. "The files?"

Benedict reached slowly into his briefcase, withdrawing the secure folder. He held it up, letting Flintly see it clearly in the fading afternoon light. "Unredacted Jennings files. Everything you asked for."

"Toss it over," Flintly instructed, keeping his distance.

"Not until I see Paisley."

Flintly chuckled. "You're not in a position to negotiate, Astor."

"Neither are you," Benedict replied calmly. "You need these files. I need Paisley. An even exchange."

Something flickered across Flintly's face. "She's not here."

Benedict had expected as much, but the confirmation still sent ice through his veins. "Where?"

"Safe," Flintly repeated. "She'll remain that way if you cooperate. The files, please."

Benedict made a show of hesitating, of internal struggle, before tossing the folder. It landed at Flintly's feet, the documents secure in their protective sleeve.

Flintly picked it up without taking his eyes or gun off Benedict. "Wise choice."

"Now Paisley," Benedict insisted.

"All in good time." Flintly tucked the folder under his arm. "First, I need to verify these aren't more of your sanitized versions."

"They're not."

"Forgive me if I don't take your word for it." Flintly gestured toward the storage unit with his gun. "Inside, please. We'll review them together."

Benedict's instincts screamed warning. Entering the confined space would put him at a significant disadvantage. But if Paisley was inside...

"Is she in there?" he asked, taking a careful step forward.

"Would I tell you if she was?" Flintly countered, his smile turning predatory. "Inside, Astor. Don't make me ask again."

Benedict complied, moving toward the unit. He heard Tanner's voice in his earpiece, a low murmur of concern.

Behind him, Flintly tossed a key to the padlock, and it clanged as it hit the cement floor by Benedict's foot.

"Open it."

Instead of arguing, Benedict did as instructed. The rolling door of Unit 27 raised, revealing shadows beyond. Benedict ducked under it, his eyes adjusting quickly to the dim interior. The space was largely empty—some cardboard boxes stacked against one wall, a folding table in the center with a laptop, a metal chair.

No Paisley.

Flintly followed him inside, keeping the gun trained on Benedict's back. "Hands where I can see them," he instructed. "Turn around slowly."

Benedict complied, raising his hands to shoulder height as he turned to face Flintly.

"Where is she?" Benedict asked again, his voice betraying none of the fear coiling in his gut.

"So single-minded." Flintly moved to the laptop, keeping the gun aimed at Benedict as he placed the folder beside it. He stood between Benedict and the exit to the storage unit. "She really has you wrapped around her finger, doesn't she? Leads you around by your dick? The great Benedict Astor, reduced to an errand boy for a woman."

"If you've hurt her—"

"You'll what?" Flintly interrupted, his attention split between the folder and Benedict. "Kill me? Doubt it. Destroy me professionally? Been there, done that." His smile turned bitter. "You took everything from me years ago, Astor. My career, my reputation, my future. Did you think there wouldn't be consequences?"

"I caught you selling client information," Benedict replied evenly. "You destroyed yourself."

Flintly's expression hardened. "I made one mistake. A single lapse in judgment. And you ensured I would never work in this industry again."

"Until Blackwater hired you."

"Yes." Flintly's smile returned. "They've been quite good to me." He opened the folder, his satisfaction evident as he began examining the documents. "Excellent," he murmured. "The complete Jennings files. These will be quite useful."

"I've kept my end of the bargain," Benedict said, maintaining his position. "Now keep yours. Where. Is. She?"

Flintly looked up from the documents, studying Benedict. "You know, I never understood why Carson trusted you so completely. What made you so special? But now I see it. You're willing to sacrifice everything for the people you care about. Even company secrets. Even your own safety." He gestured with the gun. "It's admirable, in a pathetic sort of way."

"Where, Flintly?"

"Not here. Did you really think I'd bring her to the exchange? Keep all my leverage in one place?" He chuckled. "I'm not an amateur."

"Where?"

"Somewhere secure. Somewhere you'll never find her without my help." Flintly's expression turned calculating. "Which presents us with a dilemma. I have what I need from you. What possible reason do I have to tell you where she is?"

Benedict had anticipated this betrayal. Had counted on it, in fact. "Because you want me to suffer," he said simply. "And killing me now would be too quick, too merciful."

Something flashed in Flintly's eyes; recognition, perhaps, of having his psychology so accurately read. "Very good," he acknowledged. "Though not entirely correct. I do want you to suffer, Astor. But not just emotionally. I want you destroyed professionally. Personally. Completely."

"Like you were."

"Precisely." Flintly nodded toward the folder. "These files are just the beginning."

The next time Flintly looked down to read the folder, Benedict tapped his earpiece multiple times.

"Well, I suppose I left out one little tidbit." Flintly shut the laptop and retrained the gun on Benedict. "I want you to suffer, yes. But..." He cocked the gun. "I want you dead more."

Two shots rang out in rapid succession. The first caught Flintly in the shoulder, spinning him halfway around. The second struck his hand, sending the gun clattering to the floor. Flintly collapsed against the table, blood spreading across his expensive shirt.

Tanner stepped into view, his weapon still trained on Flintly, who whimpered and moaned on the floor.

"Clear," Tanner announced after checking the perimeter. "No witnesses. No cameras."

Benedict nodded his acknowledgment. "Thanks."

He approached Flintly cautiously and kicked the fallen gun well out of reach. He knelt to check the wounds, serious but not life-threatening. Exactly as intended. Tanner's aim, as always, had been perfect.

"Where is she?" Benedict demanded.

Flintly laughed through gritted teeth. "You think this changes anything?"

Benedict grabbed Flintly's injured shoulder, applying just enough pressure to draw a hiss of pain. "I think you're going to tell me where Paisley is. Or the next bullet goes somewhere more permanent."

"You won't kill me," Flintly gasped. "Not until you know where she is."

"There are degrees of pain between life and death," Benedict said, his voice devoid of emotion. "He's intimately familiar with all of them." Benedict nodded to Tanner, who grinned in a way that made Benedict glad he was an ally and a friend.

Something like fear flickered in Flintly's eyes for the first time. "You wouldn't."

"For her?" Benedict leaned closer, his voice dropping to whisper in Flintly's ear. "I would burn this city to the ground twice over."

Tanner moved to secure the exit, his massive silhouette blocking the doorway as he checked outside. His presence alone was enough to make Flintly's resolve waver.

"Last chance," Benedict said, tilting his head. "Where is my woman?"

Flintly's expression shifted, calculation replacing fear as he weighed his options. "Insurance p-policy," he managed. "Phone. Left pocket."

Benedict reached into Flintly's jacket, retrieving a smartphone. The screen was locked, but a notification was visible: *Temperature 110 degrees.*

"What is this?" Benedict demanded, showing Flintly the screen.

"Clock's ticking, Astor. Your *woman* will likely die from heat exposure by then."

"What have you done?" Benedict grabbed Flintly's injured hand and squeezed, blood gushing out of the wound.

Flintly screamed.

"Fucking shipping container," Flintly gasped. "Standard cargo unit. She's been baking in the sun."

"Where?" Benedict pressed harder on Flintly's wound, and the man shrieked louder.

"Coordinates on the phone. Unlock code 7294." Flintly's breathing was becoming labored when Benedict let go. "But even if you find her, you'll never reach her in time. Not without me."

"Why would I need you?" Benedict asked, already unlocking the phone.

"I know where the key is," Flintly's smile was ghastly through the pain. "Kill me, and she dies."

Benedict glanced at Tanner, who nodded. They needed Flintly alive, at least until they reached Paisley.

"Patch him up," Benedict instructed, stepping back to allow Tanner access. "He's coming with us."

Tanner produced a field medical kit from his tactical vest. He worked silently, stemming the bleeding from Flintly's shoulder with a pressure bandage.

Benedict focused on the phone, finding the coordinates stored in a navigation app. They led to a shipping yard on the East River—at least thirty minutes away in current traffic.

"Well?" Tanner asked as he finished securing Flintly's wounds.

"Fuck. Fuck! The temperature is 110," Benedict replied, already heading for the door. "We need to move. Now. She's probably already lost consciousness."

Tanner hauled Flintly to his feet, ignoring the man's cry of pain. "Walk or be dragged," he growled. "Your choice."

They moved quickly through the storage facility, Benedict leading the way with Tanner half-supporting, half-dragging Flintly behind him. The security guard had been neutralized—Benedict didn't ask how—allowing them unimpeded access to Tanner's truck.

"Back seat," Tanner instructed, shoving Flintly into the vehicle. "Try anything fucker, and your other shoulder matches."

Benedict took the passenger seat, already plotting the fastest route to the shipping yard. Forty minutes. Less now. They'd need every second.

As Tanner accelerated onto the main road, lights flashing and sirens wailing from the hidden police package installed in the truck, Benedict found himself doing something he'd never done before: praying.

Not to any god or higher power, but to Paisley herself. To her strength, her resourcefulness, her will to survive. To the connection between them that had somehow transcended twelve years of denial and a month of secrets.

Hold on, he thought desperately. *I'm coming.*

CHAPTER THIRTEEN

PAISLEY

PAISLEY WOKE TO A SCORCHING HEAT THAT SENT PANIC coursing through her veins. The shipping container, which had been uncomfortably cool just hours before, now felt like the inside of an oven. Sweat poured from her body, her clothes sticking to her skin as if she'd been caught in a summer downpour.

She pushed herself up, a wave of dizziness threatening to topple her back to the metal floor. The surface beneath her palm burned, and she yanked her hand away with a hiss. The entire container had become a metal coffin, baking in what must be direct sunlight.

"God," she gasped, her throat painfully dry. Her words came out as a rasp, barely audible even in the silent container.

The concussion made every movement amplify the throbbing in her head. The heat made it exponentially worse. Paisley forced herself to focus through the pain.

The temperature was dangerously high and climbing. The air quality seemed to be deteriorating, not to mention stifling. She couldn't remember the last time she'd had water, but her throat was dry, her lips cracked. There was no way to tell how long she'd been in the container. But judging by the intensity of the heat, it must be past midday.

Paisley peeled off her outer shirt, leaving just her sweat-soaked tank top. The momentary relief was negligible against the oppressive heat. She stayed away from the metal if she could manage, choosing to sit on the broken palettes instead. Splinters were better than being cooked alive on the metal.

"Think, Paisley," she muttered.

She was trapped in a shipping container that was rapidly becoming a death trap. The heat was the immediate threat. Heat stroke would claim her soon enough.

She needed to cool down and conserve energy.

And, she needed to find a way out, or at least a way to survive until help came.

If help was coming at all.

Paisley shook the thought away. Benedict would be looking for her. She had to believe that. There was nothing else to hold on to. Not like the idea of Benedict. The thought of him would be her lifeline in that metal hell.

She crawled to the rusted hinge she'd been working on before, only to recoil instantly.

"Shit!" The metal was hot enough to blister skin. Her makeshift tool, the wooden shard from the pallet, lay a few feet away. She retrieved it, using it as a barrier between her hands and the scorching metal as she tried to continue her work on the hinge.

The wood slipped, digging a splinter into her palm. Paisley cursed, fatigue and heat making her clumsy. She sucked at the wound, the coppery taste of blood mixing with the salt of her sweat.

She couldn't control the heat. Couldn't control the passage of time. Couldn't control whether Benedict would find her before it was too late.

But she could control her breathing. Her thoughts. Her efforts to survive.

Paisley closed her eyes, trying to steady herself against a wave of nausea. The heat was affecting her more severely now. She recognized the symptoms of heat exhaustion setting in. Dizziness. Headache.

Racing heart. She needed water desperately, but there was none to be found.

Her thoughts turned to Carson. To the secrets she'd kept from him. The lies she'd told, justified by the belief that she was protecting him. If she died here, he would never know the truth. Would never understand why she'd betrayed his trust. Would be left only with questions and confusion and anger.

And Benedict...

Pain that had nothing to do with the heat or her concussion twisted in her chest. They'd wasted so much time. Twelve years of wanting each other from a distance, only one month of finally being together. It wasn't enough. Not nearly enough.

"I'm not dying here," she growled through clenched teeth.

With renewed determination, Paisley pushed herself back to her feet, fighting the wave of dizziness that threatened to send her crashing to the floor. She needed to be methodical. To think through her options even as her brain felt like it was baking inside her skull.

Her eyes adjusted to the dim light filtering through the ventilation slats, and she began a more careful inspection of the container. There had to be something she'd missed. Some weakness in the structure she could exploit.

Near the corner furthest from the doors, she noticed a slight discoloration in the metal—perhaps rust or a manufacturing defect. She stumbled toward it, her legs feeling increasingly unreliable. As she drew closer, she felt it: the faintest wisp of cooler air against her sweat-slicked skin.

A seam in the metal, barely perceptible, but allowing a trickle of air to enter from outside.

Paisley pressed her face against it gratefully, the marginally cooler air a blessing against her feverish skin. She breathed deeply, trying to fill her lungs with less super-heated air. It wasn't much, but it was something. A small advantage in a situation with precious few.

She stripped off her tank top, leaving only her bra, and soaked the fabric with her sweat. She pressed it against her face, her neck, trying to cool her pulse points.

"Wrists, neck, forehead," she murmured, remembering the advice from when she'd gone hiking one summer with some friends in college.

Muscle cramps seized her calf, and Paisley bit back a cry of pain. She massaged the knotted muscle with shaking hands. Her heart pounded in her chest, too fast, too hard, as if trying to escape its cage of ribs.

She slid down the wall, positioning herself near the small air seam, trying to conserve what little energy remained. The metal floor burned through the fabric of her jeans, but she lacked the strength to remain standing.

Time became fluid, stretching and contracting in her heat-addled mind. She drifted in and out of awareness, her thoughts fracturing into disconnected fragments. Carson's laugh. Benedict's hands. The taste of coffee in the morning. The smell of her mother's perfume.

Paisley rolled onto her back, staring up at the dark ceiling of the container. Was this how it ended? Would she die alone in a metal box, baked alive under the summer sun?

The unfairness of it tore a sob from her parched throat.

Through the haze of heat and dehydration, a noise penetrated her consciousness. At first, she thought she was hallucinating. A clanking sound, metal on metal, coming from outside the container.

Paisley held her breath, straining to hear past the pounding of her own heart.

There it was again. Unmistakable. Something, or someone, was at the container doors.

Hope and fear surged through her in equal measure. It could be rescue, Benedict finding her somehow Or it could be Flintly, returning to finish what he'd started.

She forced her leaden limbs into motion, crawling toward the wooden shard she'd dropped. Her fingers closed around it.

The sounds grew louder. A metallic scraping, then a definitive click as the padlock disengaged.

Paisley pushed herself up against the wall next to the doors, her makeshift weapon clutched in a white-knuckled grip. She tried to stand but her legs would no longer support her weight. She remained crouched, her breathing shallow, every muscle tensed despite her exhaustion.

Light. Blindingly bright, it spilled into the container as the door began to slide open. Heat rushed out in a visible wave, like the blast from an oven door.

Paisley squinted against the sudden brightness, raising one trembling hand to shield her eyes. A silhouette stood in the doorway, backlit by the sun, features impossible to discern.

The wooden shard slipped from her grasp as darkness crowded the edges of her vision. Dehydration, heat exhaustion, and sheer relief combined to push her toward unconsciousness.

Before the darkness claimed her, one last conscious thought flickered through her mind:

Please let it be Benedict.

CHAPTER FOURTEEN

BENEDICT

BENEDICT SAT BESIDE PAISLEY'S UNCONSCIOUS FORM, watching the gentle rise and fall of her chest beneath the soft cotton sheets of his bed. The medical equipment Dr. Nikelson had left behind hummed quietly; an IV stand delivering fluids to combat severe dehydration, a heart monitor with its reassuring steady beep, an oxygen saturation sensor clipped to her finger.

He hadn't slept. Couldn't sleep. Every time he closed his eyes, he saw her as he'd found her, crumpled against the wall of that metal coffin, her skin burning with fever, her breathing shallow and rapid. He'd never known terror like that moment when he thought he might have been too late.

Flintly's fucking coordinates had nearly cost Paisley her life. The phone had led to an empty shipping container, a decoy meant to waste precious minutes while Paisley baked in another location entirely. If Benedict hadn't recognized the shipping logo in the background of the image Flintly had sent when Paisley had awoken, if he hadn't trusted his instincts over Flintly's misdirection...

It also helped that Tanner used subtle tactics to make Flintly confirm the shipping dock they were heading to after finding the decoy was the real one.

There had been minimal screaming.

Benedict's hand trembled as he reached out to brush a damp curl from Paisley's face. Dr. Nikelson had assured him that she would recover fully with rest and hydration, but the memory of carrying her limp body from that super-heated container haunted him. Her skin had been scorching to the touch, her pulse racing but weak, her breathing erratic.

He had never felt so helpless. He, who prided himself on anticipating every threat, who had built his career on control and calculation, had nearly lost everything because he'd underestimated an enemy's desperation.

Because he'd fallen in love.

The beeping of the heart monitor changed as Paisley stirred, her eyelids fluttering. Benedict leaned forward. Her eyes opened slowly, unfocused at first, then gradually sharpening as she took in her surroundings.

"Ben?" Her voice was a rasp, barely audible.

Relief crashed through him with such force that for a moment he couldn't speak. He reached for the glass of water on the nightstand, gently supporting her head as he held it to her lips.

"Small sips," he murmured, his own voice rough from lack of sleep.

She obeyed, wincing as the cool liquid touched her parched throat. When she'd had enough, Benedict set the glass aside, his fingers lingering against her cheek.

"You found me," she whispered, leaning into his touch.

"I did," he replied.

Paisley's eyes searched his face. "How long was I out?" she asked.

"Twenty-six hours since I found you. You've been drifting in and out." Benedict's thumb traced circles on the back of her hand where the IV needle wasn't inserted. "Dr. Nikelson says you'll make a full recovery, but it'll take time. Severe heat exhaustion, dehydration, and that concussion Flintly gave you. Your body needs rest."

At the mention of Flintly's name, Paisley's expression hardened. "Where is he?"

Benedict hesitated, weighing truth against protection. But he'd promised her no more secrets, even when those secrets were meant to shield her.

"He escaped," he admitted reluctantly. "When we found you, getting you medical attention took priority. He got away while Tanner and I were unlocking the storage container. I stayed with you while Tanner went to bring his truck closer. I was too busy making sure you were still alive, that he slipped away. Tanner searched the immediate area, but Flintly was gone by then. He must have had a vehicle waiting nearby."

Paisley tried to sit up, wincing. Benedict gently pressed her back against the pillows.

"Easy," he cautioned. "You're still recovering."

"He can't just get away with this," she said, frustration evident in her voice despite its weakness. "He'll try again, Ben. Maybe not against me, but against you, against Carson, against the company."

"I know." Benedict ran a hand through his hair, disheveled from the hours of anxious vigil. "Part of me wants to let him disappear—watching what he did to you, thinking I might lose you..." He paused, struggling to maintain his composure. "But you're right. As long as Flintly's out there, none of us are safe."

Paisley's fingers tightened around his. "Then we find him."

Benedict studied her face. The determination in her eyes despite the pallor of her skin, the stubborn set of her jaw that reminded him so much of Carson. The Crest siblings shared that same indomitable will, that refusal to back down even when the odds were stacked against them.

It was one of the many things he loved about her.

"First, you need to recover," he said firmly. "Flintly won't make his next move immediately. He'll be regrouping, adapting his strategy. That gives us time." Benedict spared a small smile. "Also, there's the fact that Tanner shot him twice."

"Remind me to buy him some nice scotch," Paisley's expression shifted from amusement to concern, "does Carson know what happened?"

Benedict shook his head. "He's been completely absorbed with Kinsley Ellis's reputation rehabilitation. They've been practically inseparable for the past week; meetings, interviews, public appearances."

"So he has no idea his sister was abducted and almost killed?" There was no accusation in her tone, just a wry observation.

"No." Benedict's lips curved in a humorless smile. "And right now, that might be for the best. Carson's... different lately. More focused on Kinsley than company matters. I've never seen him like this with a client."

"Or with anyone since Emma," Paisley added softly.

Benedict nodded, remembering the way Carson had changed after his fiancée's death. He'd become harder, more driven, less willing to connect. Until Kinsley Ellis had stumbled into his life, looking at him like he was her salvation.

"We should tell him," Paisley said after a moment of silence.

"We will," Benedict agreed. "But I think we should wait a little longer. we need a better understanding of Flintly's next move. Carson has enough on his plate right now, and..."

"And you want to know where Flintly is before bringing Carson in," Paisley finished for him. "So he doesn't do anything rash."

"Exactly." Benedict reached for his phone. "Which means we need Penn."

Twenty minutes later, Penn arrived at the penthouse, his arms laden with equipment and his expression shifting from neutral to shock when he saw Paisley's condition.

"Jesus," he muttered, setting down his gear on Benedict's dining table. "Flintly did this to you?"

Paisley nodded, now propped up on the couch in the living room where Benedict had insisted on carrying her despite her protests that she could walk. "Locked me in a shipping container during the hottest day of the year."

Penn's normally twitchy demeanor stilled, his gaze sharpening. Behind the social awkwardness and technical brilliance, Penn possessed a streak of ruthlessness when those he considered his own were threatened.

"We'll find him," Penn said simply. "I'll make damn sure of it."

He began unpacking his equipment. Specialized laptops, external drives, networking gear that Benedict suspected was several generations ahead of what was commercially available. Within minutes, Penn had established connections to his systems at Crest Strategies, his fingers flying across multiple keyboards simultaneously.

"I've been tracking Blackwater since all of this started," he explained, not looking up from his screens. "I installed protocols to flag any unusual access patterns."

"And?" Benedict prompted, settling beside Paisley on the couch, his arm protectively around her shoulders.

"Flintly's good, but not as good as he thinks he is." Penn's lips curved in a small, satisfied smile. "He's been accessing Blackwater systems remotely, probably uploading the files you gave him and communicating with his handlers."

"Can you trace him?" Paisley asked, leaning forward despite Benedict's gentle restraining hand.

"Not his physical location yet," Penn admitted. "He's bouncing his signal through multiple proxies. But I've identified his digital signature. I'm running algorithms now to narrow down his location based on connection timing and data packet analysis."

"What can you tell us about his activities within Blackwater's system?" Benedict asked.

Penn's expression grew more focused as he pulled up a series of data visualizations. "He's accessing files related to Crest Strategies' clients, particularly those with political connections. And..." Penn paused, his eyebrows drawing together. "He's been researching identity creation protocols."

"He's planning to disappear," Benedict concluded.

"Or establish a new identity for extended surveillance," Penn countered. "The pattern suggests preparation for a long-term operation, not an immediate exit."

Paisley shifted against Benedict's side, her voice stronger than it had been earlier. "When I was in that container, he talked about his plan. About framing Carson for my murder, about destroying Crest Strategies so Blackwater could acquire what was left."

"The timeline for that kind of corporate takeover would be months, not days," Benedict observed.

Penn nodded. "This would all suggest he's planning something with a longer horizon. The digital breadcrumbs point to preparation, not immediate action."

"Which means we have time," Paisley said, her hand finding Benedict's and squeezing. "Time to find him before he makes his next move."

"Time to protect Carson while he's distracted with Kinsley," Benedict added, the irony not lost on him. For years, he'd been the one distracted by his feelings for Paisley, unable to act on them because of his loyalty to Carson. Now Carson was experiencing something similar with Kinsley, creating a window of opportunity they couldn't afford to waste.

"Speaking of Carson," Penn said, glancing up from his screens, "I've never seen him like this. Tanner made a comment about how Kinsley looked in a specific dress the other day, and your brother actually growled. It was fucking hilarious."

Paisley's lips curved in amusement. "Sounds serious."

"He denied it when James mentioned it," Penn continued, returning his attention to his data analysis.

"Carson deserves to be happy," Paisley said, snuggling closer to Benedict. "After Emma, I wasn't sure he'd ever let himself care about someone again."

"All the more reason to handle Flintly ourselves," Benedict replied. "At least until we understand exactly what he's planning."

Penn's keyboard clacking paused as he looked up at them both. "You realize you'll have to tell him eventually. About Flintly and about..." he gestured between them, "...this."

"We will," Benedict assured him. "Once we take out Flintly."

"And after I'm fully recovered," Paisley added. "I don't want him seeing me like this. He'll explode. We'll all be casualties in it too."

Penn nodded, returning to his work. "The tracking elements in those files you gave Flintly should activate when he accesses them from a static location. I've set up alerts to notify us immediately when that happens."

"In the meantime," Benedict said, "we monitor Blackwater's activities, track Flintly's digital footprint, and prepare for his next move."

"I can help," Paisley insisted. "Even from here, while I'm recovering. I spent weeks communicating with him as Marcus. I understand how he thinks, what motivates him."

Benedict wanted to object, to insist she focus solely on recovery, but he knew better than to underestimate her determination. Instead, he nodded. "Your insight could be invaluable. But you rest when I say rest, understood?"

The look she gave him was equal parts affection and exasperation. "Yes, sir."

Penn continued working for several hours, setting up monitoring systems and explaining the tracking protocols he'd implemented. As evening fell, he gathered his equipment, leaving behind one specialized laptop connected to his systems at Crest Strategies.

"This will alert you to any activity from Flintly's digital signature," he explained as he prepared to leave. "I've programmed it to notify all three of us simultaneously if it detects anything suspicious."

"Thank you, Penn," Paisley said sincerely. "For everything."

Penn shuffled awkwardly. "You're part of Crest Strategies," he said simply, as if that explained everything. In a way, it did. Despite their different roles, different backgrounds, different temperaments, they were bound by loyalty to the company and to each other.

After Penn left, Benedict helped Paisley back to the bedroom. Her steps were unsteady, her body still recovering.

"I'm not an invalid," she protested as he lowered her gently onto the bed.

"No," he agreed, sitting beside her. "You're the strongest person I know. But even you need time to heal."

Paisley's expression softened. She reached up to touch his face, her fingers tracing the stubble on his jaw. "You need to rest too. You look terrible."

A surprised laugh escaped him. "Always so flattering."

"I mean it, Ben. You can't protect anyone if you collapse from exhaustion."

He captured her hand, pressing a kiss to her palm. "I'll rest. But first, let Dr. Nikelson's medicine do its work. She left something to help you sleep through the night."

Paisley didn't argue as he administered the prescribed dose. Within minutes, her eyelids began to droop, the medication drawing her toward much-needed sleep.

"Stay with me," she murmured, fighting to keep her eyes open.

Benedict stretched out beside her on the bed, careful not to disturb the IV line. "Always."

"We'll find him," she whispered, her voice fading as sleep claimed her.

"Yeah, we will," he echoed, watching as she drifted off.

Benedict remained beside her, listening to her steady breathing, feeling the warmth of her body against his.

He'd nearly lost her.

The thought was unbearable.

CHAPTER FIFTEEN

BENEDICT

BENEDICT STARED AT THE SURVEILLANCE PHOTOS ON THE screen, his jaw tightening as Flintly's face came into focus. Penn's tracking algorithms had finally paid off. Three weeks of digital breadcrumbs leading to a remote cabin upstate, far from the city's watchful eyes. The perfect hiding place for a man with too many enemies.

"You're sure it's him?" Benedict asked, though he already knew the answer. Penn's work was never less than precise.

"Facial recognition is 99.8% positive," Penn replied through the secure line. "He's been there for six days. Purchased supplies in a nearby town using a false identity, but his biometric markers are unmistakable."

Benedict nodded, studying the cabin's layout on the satellite imagery. Isolated. Single access road. No neighbors for miles. Ideal for what needed to be done.

"Send everything to my secure server," he instructed. "And Penn? This conversation never happened."

"What conversation?" Penn replied before disconnecting.

Benedict closed the laptop and leaned back in his chair, allowing himself a moment of grim satisfaction. For three weeks, he'd been waiting for this. The opportunity to eliminate the threat Flintly posed to Paisley, to Carson, to everything he held dear. The memory of Paisley in that fucking shipping container fueled nightmares that woke Benedict in cold sweats, his heart racing until he felt Paisley's warm body beside him, safe and alive.

He glanced toward the bedroom where she slept peacefully now. In just a few days after her rescue, she'd recovered remarkably. Dr. Nikelson had called it a testament to her resilience; physically, at least, Paisley had healed. The nightmares that occasionally gripped her were another matter.

Benedict moved through the penthouse that now bore unmistakable signs of Paisley's presence; her books stacked on the coffee table, her favorite mug in the dish rack, her cardigan draped over his office chair. What had begun as a temporary arrangement had evolved without discussion into something more permanent. Neither had mentioned her returning to her own apartment. Neither wanted to.

It felt right having her here. As if she belonged.

He checked the secure phone they used to communicate with Carson during his recovery. His best friend, his business partner, the man whose trust he'd betrayed in the most fundamental way had gone through his own version of hell not two weeks after Benedict got Paisley back. He'd been shot in his own apartment while protecting Kinsley. The irony wasn't lost on Benedict. While he'd been consumed with Paisley's safety, Carson had been fighting his own battles, unaware of the secrets being kept from him.

God, when had Benedict become such a shitty friend?

They'd visited Carson yesterday at his apartment, where Kinsley had been a near-constant presence during his recovery. The distance Benedict and Paisley maintained in his presence had become second nature. No lingering touches, no intimate glances, nothing to betray the relationship they'd hidden for over two months now.

The deception weighed on them both, but they'd agreed to wait until Carson had physically recovered before adding emotional stress to his plate. At least, that's what they told themselves. The truth was the longer they waited, the harder it was to motivate themselves to tell him.

Benedict returned to his office, making preparations for the confrontation with Flintly. He contacted Tanner, arranging for backup and cleanup without explicitly stating his intentions. Some things didn't need to be said between men like them. Tanner would understand what was required.

He was so absorbed in his planning that he didn't hear Paisley approach until her voice broke the silence.

"You found him."

Benedict turned to find her standing in the doorway, wearing one of his t-shirts that hung to mid-thigh, her curls tousled from sleep. Even now, the sight of her stole his breath.

"Yes," he admitted, seeing no point in denial. She'd always been able to read him too well.

"When do we leave?" She entered the office fully, moving to stand beside him as she scanned the images on his desk.

"*We* don't," Benedict replied, his tone making it clear the matter wasn't open for discussion. "I'm handling this with Tanner. You're staying here."

Paisley's expression hardened. "The hell I am."

"Paisley—"

"Don't 'Paisley' me in that tone." She planted her hands on his desk, leaning forward. "He locked me in a shipping container to die, Benedict. He gave me this." She gestured to the faint scar at her temple where Flintly had struck her. "I deserve to be there when you confront him."

Benedict stood, his height allowing him to tower over her, though the intimidation tactic had never worked on Paisley. "It's too dangerous. If something went wrong—"

"Then it goes wrong for both of us," she interrupted, her eyes flashing with that Crest stubbornness he'd come to both admire and find infuriating. "I'm not some delicate flower you need to protect, Ben. I thought we established that when I survived being baked alive in a metal box."

The memory made his jaw clench. "That's exactly why I won't risk you again. I almost lost you once. I won't—"

"You don't get to make that decision for me," she cut him off, stepping closer until they were inches apart. "We're in this together. We agreed. No more secrets, no more unilateral decisions."

"This is different," Benedict insisted, though he could already feel his resolve weakening under her determined gaze.

"No, it's not. Carson's getting better. He's healing. We've been waiting to tell him about us until he's stronger, but we've also been waiting for closure with Flintly. I need this, Ben. I need to look him in the eye and let him know he failed. That we survived. That we're stronger together than he could ever be alone."

Benedict studied her face. He knew that look. Knew she wouldn't back down. And despite his protective instincts screaming in protest, he knew she was right.

"Fine," he conceded finally. "But you follow my lead. You stay behind me. You wear body armor. And if I say we leave, we leave. No arguments."

A triumphant smile curved her lips. "Agreed."

"I mean it, Paisley. One sign of trouble and—"

His words were cut off as she closed the distance between them, lungeing across the desk. Her mouth found his in a kiss that ignited instantly. Three weeks of shared space, of healing, of carefully navigating Carson's recovery had created a pressure between them that sought release.

Benedict's hands found her waist, fingers digging into the soft flesh as he pulled her against him. Paisley responded by pressing closer, her body arching into his with a familiarity that still amazed him. His mouth left hers to trail down her neck, teeth grazing the sensitive spot that always made her gasp.

"You're impossible," he murmured against her skin. "Stubborn. Reckless."

"You love it," she replied, her fingers tangling in his hair to pull him back up for another searing kiss.

He did. God help him, he loved everything about her—her defiance, her courage, her refusal to be sheltered. Even when it terrified him.

Their argument dissolved into desperate touches, clothes hastily discarded as they collided against his desk. Papers scattered to the floor as Benedict lifted her onto the polished surface, his hands pushing her thighs apart. Paisley's head fell back as his mouth traced a path down her body, his destination clear.

"Ben," she gasped as his tongue found her center, her hands gripping the edge of the desk for support.

He took his time, using his mouth and fingers to drive her to the edge repeatedly before backing away, a sweet torture that had her cursing his name between pleas for release. If he couldn't protect her from danger, he would at least worship her body until she forgot everything but the pleasure he gave her.

When he finally allowed her to come, her cry echoed through the penthouse, her body shaking. Benedict rose, positioning himself between her trembling thighs, his eyes locked on hers.

"Do you want me to get a condom?" He asked, praying she said no.

"Fuck, no."

Even better.

"Mine," he growled, the word escaping before he could stop it. He pushed all the way into her.

Paisley's eyes darkened. She wrapped her legs around his waist, pulling him deeper. "Yours," she agreed. "Fucking yours."

He established a rhythm that bordered on punishing, each thrust a physical declaration of his need for her, his fear of losing her, his acceptance that she was his equal in this as in all things.

Paisley matched him move for move, her nails leaving crescent marks on his shoulders as she pulled him closer, demanded more. The desk creaked beneath them, solid mahogany straining.

"Look at me," Benedict commanded as he felt her approaching another climax, needing to see the moment pleasure overtook her.

Her eyes locked on his, vulnerability and trust and fierce desire all mingled in her gaze. It undid him. They came together, her name a prayer on his lips as he emptied himself inside her, her body clenching around him as if reluctant to ever let go.

Afterward, Benedict's hands gentled, tenderly stroking her back as he pulled out of her. With two fingers, he swiped up her folds, gathering the moisture and pressing it into her mouth. She licked every part off him.

"Fuck." He growled, grinning as he rested his forehead against hers.

"Exactly."

It took a while before either of them pulled themselves together. When they did, Benedict checked his phone.

"Tanner says we leave at dawn. He's already preparing."

Paisley nodded, pressing a soft kiss to the corner of his mouth. "Thank you for not leaving me behind."

"As if I could stop you," he replied, though they both knew he could have. That his concession was a choice, not a defeat.

She smiled, the expression lighting her eyes in a way that made his chest tighten. "I'd just follow you anyway."

"I know."

———

THE NEXT MORNING, THE CABIN CAME INTO VIEW AS THEY rounded a bend in the narrow dirt road, a nondescript structure nestled among tall pines. From the passenger seat, Paisley studied it through binoculars, her expression revealing nothing of the emotions Benedict knew must be churning beneath her calm exterior.

"Someone is visible through the east window," she reported. "Moving around the main room. Looks like Flintly."

Benedict nodded, pulling their SUV to a stop in a clearing half a mile from the cabin. Tanner's truck was already there, its owner emerging from the tree line as they exited their vehicle.

"Perimeter's clear," Tanner reported, his massive frame moving with surprising stealth through the underbrush. "No booby traps, no surveillance equipment. He's not expecting company."

"Overconfident," Benedict observed. "Good."

Tanner's gaze shifted to Paisley, then back to Benedict, a silent question in his eyes. Benedict gave a slight nod. Yes, she knew what might happen here today. Yes, she was prepared for it.

"Comms check," Benedict said, activating the earpiece they each wore.

"Clear," Paisley replied.

"Five by five," Tanner confirmed.

Tanner opened the bed of his truck, revealing an arsenal of weapons and tactical gear. Benedict selected a matte black handgun with a suppressor attachment, checking it before holstering it beneath his jacket. Tanner was already armed. He'd arrived ready for what needed to be done.

Paisley stepped forward. "Should I take one?"

"Know how to use it?" Tanner asked, raising a brow.

"No."

"Then fuck no." He shut the bed of the truck.

"Dickweed," Paisley muttered, wrinkling her nose at him.

Tanner just rolled his eyes. "Cry me a fucking river, Baby Crest."

"Careful. She's mine, and you'll watch your fucking mouth when you talk to her."

"Whatever," Tanner said, shrugging. "Your as bad as her brother is with all this lovey-dovey shit."

"Watch out. You'll be next, Whitney," Paisley said, hands on her hips.

"Yeah, when fucking hell freezes the fuck over." He glared at her. "I don't do that shit. I fuck. That's it. And if you—"

"Can we focus? Let's remember the plan," Benedict interrupted, narrowing his gaze at Tanner. "Tanner takes the rear entrance. We approach from the front. We'll breach and clear. Paisley, you stay behind me at all times."

She nodded. "Got it."

They moved through the forest, approaching the cabin from different angles. Through his earpiece, Benedict heard Tanner's steady breathing as he took position at the rear door. Paisley remained close behind him, her footsteps nearly as quiet as his own.

At the cabin's front porch, Benedict paused, listening. Inside, a chair scraped across wooden floors.

Benedict met Paisley's gaze, giving her one last chance to stay behind. She shook her head minutely. With a resigned nod, he turned back to the door.

"In position," Tanner's voice came through the earpiece.

"Execute on my mark," Benedict replied softly. "Three. Two. One. Mark."

The synchronized breach was textbook perfect. Benedict at the front door, Tanner at the rear, both entering simultaneously with weapons drawn. Paisley followed Benedict inside, staying in his shadow as promised.

Flintly sat at a cluttered desk, his back to the front door, typing furiously on a laptop surrounded by stacks of papers and external hard drives. At the sound of the breach, he spun around, his expression shifting from shock to a strange, resigned amusement as he recognized his visitors.

"Astor," he said, leaning back in his chair. "I was wondering when you'd find me."

Benedict kept his weapon trained on Flintly's chest. "Hands where I can see them."

Flintly complied, raising his hands to shoulder height with a wince. His injured shoulder, the one Tanner had shot, along with his right hand, were bandaged. His gaze shifted to Paisley, who had moved to stand behind Benedict's right shoulder.

"Ms. Crest," Flintly acknowledged. "You're looking well for someone who should be dead."

Benedict felt Paisley tense beside him but she remained silent.

"No witty comeback?" Flintly taunted. "No righteous indignation? I must say, I'm disappointed. After our time together in that shipping container, I expected more fire."

"Yeah, well I'm not dead. Is that what you wanted me to say you piece of shit," Paisley replied, her voice ice-cold. "You're nothing. A failed man with a pathetic grudge who couldn't even kill someone properly."

Flintly's smile tightened. "Technical difficulties. It happens. But I learned from that mistake, as you'll soon discover."

Benedict stepped further into the room, keeping himself between Flintly and Paisley. "This ends today," he said, his voice devoid of emotion. "No more threats. No more games."

"Does it?" Flintly's eyebrows rose in mock surprise. "I think you'll find this is just beginning. Did you really think I was working alone? That Blackwater wouldn't have contingencies?"

"We know about Blackwater," Benedict replied. "We know you were acting without authorization. That's why you're hiding here instead of enjoying their protection."

Something flickered in Flintly's eyes, uncertainty, perhaps. "You know nothing."

"Penn traced your communications," Paisley said, stepping out from behind Benedict despite his subtle gesture to stay back. "We know Blackwater cut ties with you after me kidnapped her. You're a liability to them now."

Flintly's composure slipped for a moment before he regained control. "So what's your plan? Kill me? Turn me over to the authorities? Neither option ends well for Crest Strategies. I've accumulated enough evidence of your unethical practices to ensure mutual destruction."

"We're not here for Crest Strategies," Benedict said, his voice dangerously soft. "We're here for Paisley."

"Ah. This is personal. How touching." His gaze shifted between them, a knowing smile spreading across his face. "I see Carson still doesn't know about your little arrangement. How do you think he'll react when he discovers his best friend has been fucking his sister behind his back?"

Benedict's expression remained impassive, though his trigger finger tightened.

"You're stalling," Benedict observed calmly. "It won't work."

Flintly leaned forward slightly. "I've prepared for this moment,

Astor. Everything I know—about you, about Carson, about your entire operation—has been secured with a dead man's switch. Kill me, and it all goes public."

"You're assuming we care about that more than seeing you pay for what you did," Paisley said, her voice steady.

"Oh, you might not, but these two do." Flintly's smile widened. "Especially with Carson recovering from that unfortunate shooting. Imagine adding this stress to his plate. The betrayal by his sister and best friend. The exposure of Crest Strategies' darker operations. It might be too much for him. Wouldn't want him ending up like his dead fiancée, now would we?"

Tanner moved silently around the room's perimeter, positioning himself behind Flintly while keeping his weapon trained on the man's back. "Your call, Ben," Tanner said.

Flintly's gaze darted to a drawer in his desk, the movement so subtle most would have missed it. Benedict didn't.

"Whatever you're thinking," Benedict warned, "don't."

"I'm merely considering my options," Flintly replied. "Perhaps we can reach an accommodation. I have information that could be valuable to Crest Strategies. Blackwater's client list, their tactics, their weaknesses. We could help each other."

"You locked me in a metal box to die," Paisley said, stepping closer despite Benedict's subtle warning. "You kidnapped me. Struck me. Left me to bake to death while you watched from a distance. And you think we'd ever trust you?"

"Business is business, Ms. Crest," Flintly replied with a shrug of his good shoulder. "Nothing personal."

"It was personal to me," Paisley countered.

"And it's personal to me," Benedict added.

Flintly must have sensed the shift in the atmosphere. The moment when negotiation became impossible. His good hand moved with surprising speed toward the desk drawer. Benedict reacted instantly, but Paisley was closer.

She lunged forward, attempting to stop Flintly's movement, but he shoved her aside. She stumbled back as Flintly's hand emerged from the drawer holding a small handgun.

Three shots rang out simultaneously. Flintly's wild shot hit at the same time both Benedict's and Tanner's bullets found their target. One through the heart. One through the head.

Flintly slumped forward, dead before he hit the desk, blood pooling beneath him and seeping into the papers scattered across its surface.

Benedict was at Paisley's side in an instant, examining the wound on her arm. "How bad?"

"Just a graze," she assured him, though her face had paled. "I'm fine."

Benedict's expression darkened as he looked from her injury to Flintly's body. "You shouldn't have moved forward. I told you to stay behind me."

"He was going for the gun," Paisley defended. "I was closer."

"And you nearly got yourself killed," Benedict replied, his voice tight.

"But I didn't." Paisley met his gaze. "We did what we came to do. It's over."

Tanner approached Flintly's body, checking for a pulse though it was clearly unnecessary. "Clean shots," he observed, glancing at Benedict. "I'll clean up."

Benedict forced himself to focus on Tanner rather than Paisley's idiotic move. "Search the cabin first. Anything related to Crest Strategies or Blackwater comes with us. Then we burn it all."

Tanner nodded, already moving to examine Flintly's laptop and the surrounding papers.

Benedict turned back to Paisley, producing a small medical kit from his pocket. "Let me see that arm."

She submitted to his ministrations, allowing him to clean and bandage the graze. Her eyes never left his face, studying his expression as he worked.

"Are you okay?" she asked, surprising him with her concern given she was the one who'd been shot.

Benedict's hands paused momentarily. "I've never killed before," he said simply.

"That's not what I asked." Her fingers found his chin, tilting his face up to meet her eyes. "Are you okay?"

"He could have killed you," Benedict said, his voice barely above a whisper. "Again. I can't—" He stopped, unable to complete the thought.

Paisley leaned forward, pressing her forehead against his. "But he didn't. We're both here. We're both alive. And he'll never threaten us again."

Benedict closed his eyes briefly, allowing himself the moment of vulnerability before the work of cleaning up Flintly's existence resumed. "I love you," he said quietly. "I would have killed him a thousand times over for what he did to you."

"I know," she replied simply. "That's why I needed to be here. To see it end. To know for certain he could never hurt either of us again."

They remained that way for a moment, foreheads touching, breathing synced, before Benedict straightened, a mask sliding back into place.

"Help Tanner gather everything related to Crest Strategies," he instructed when he'd finished with her arm. "I'll check the rest of the cabin for anything we might have missed."

For the next hour, they systematically stripped the cabin of any evidence connecting Flintly to them or their company. When they had gathered everything of value, Tanner produced several canisters of accelerant from his truck. They doused the cabin thoroughly, paying special attention to areas that might preserve DNA or other evidence. Flintly's body remained where it had fallen, surrounded by papers they'd purposely left behind to fuel the fire.

Standing outside, Benedict watched as Tanner prepared the remote ignition device. Paisley stood beside him, her expression unreadable as she gazed at the cabin that would become Dawson Flintly's funeral pyre.

"Any last words?" Tanner asked, his finger hovering over the detonator.

Benedict looked at Paisley, leaving the decision to her.

She considered for a moment, then shook her head. "He doesn't deserve them."

Tanner nodded and pressed the button. The cabin erupted in flames, the fire spreading rapidly through the accelerant-soaked structure. They watched in silence as the blaze consumed everything inside, erasing all traces of Flintly's existence and their presence.

"It'll look like an accident," Tanner observed. "Gas leak, maybe. Remote cabin, faulty equipment. Happens all the time."

Benedict nodded, his arm slipping around Paisley's waist. "We should go. The local authorities will respond to the smoke eventually."

They drove back to the city in near silence. Tanner departed with a simple nod when they reached the outskirts, his truck turning toward his own residence while Benedict continued toward the penthouse with Paisley.

It wasn't until they were safely inside, the door locked behind them, that Paisley finally spoke. "Do you think his dead man's switch was real? Will information about Crest Strategies be released?"

"Penn's already monitoring for unusual data dumps or scheduled releases," Benedict replied, removing his jacket and the shoulder holster beneath it. "If anything appears, we'll handle it."

Paisley nodded, her gaze distant as she moved toward the bedroom. "I need a shower."

Benedict watched her go, giving her the space he sensed she needed. He busied himself checking in with Penn, confirming that no suspicious activity had been detected on any of their monitored channels. By the time he'd completed the security protocols and locked away the weapons they'd returned with, Paisley had emerged from the bathroom wrapped in one of his robes, her hair damp from the shower.

She looked smaller somehow, more vulnerable than she had at the cabin. The adrenaline had worn off, leaving behind the woman who, despite her strength, had endured trauma that would have broken many others.

"Come here," Benedict said softly, opening his arms to her.

Paisley moved into his embrace without hesitation, her body melting against his. He held her tightly, one hand cradling the back of her head, the other splayed across her back to keep her close.

"It's really over," she whispered against his chest.

"Yes," he confirmed, pressing a kiss to the top of her head. "He can't hurt you—hurt us—ever again."

She tilted her face up to his, her eyes searching his. "No regrets?"

"None," Benedict replied without hesitation. "I would do it again in a heartbeat to keep you safe."

The certainty in his voice seemed to ease something in her. Paisley rose on tiptoes to press her lips to his, the kiss gentle at first, then deepening.

Benedict responded in kind, his hands moving to the belt of her robe, loosening it. As the fabric parted, revealing her bare skin beneath, his breath caught. No matter how many times he saw her like this, the effect was always the same; a mixture of desire and disbelief that she was his.

"Bed," she murmured against his lips, already working at the buttons of his shirt.

He complied, lifting her into his arms and carrying her to their bedroom.

Afterward, as they lay tangled together, heartbeats gradually slowing, bodies cooling in the dim light of early evening, Benedict's fingers traced lazy patterns on Paisley's back, his mind finally quiet after weeks of constant vigilance.

"We need to tell Carson," Paisley said eventually, her voice soft but determined. "About us. Now that Flintly's gone, we don't have that excuse anymore."

Benedict sighed, his hand stilling on her skin. "I know. His doctor's appointment is next week. If he gets cleared for normal activities, we'll tell him then."

"He's getting stronger every day," Paisley observed. "Did you notice at our last visit? His color was better. He was more alert."

"Kinsley's been good for him," Benedict acknowledged.

Paisley propped herself up on one elbow, studying his face. "Are you afraid of telling him? Really afraid, I mean."

Benedict considered the question with the honesty she deserved. "Yes," he admitted finally. "Not just of his reaction, though that's part of it. I'm afraid of making this real, Paisley. Of stepping out of the shadows where we've been living and into the light where everyone can see us."

"Because once it's real, it can be lost."

He nodded, his throat tight with emotion he rarely allowed himself to express. "I've spent my entire adult life controlling variables, anticipating threats, maintaining boundaries. With you, I've crossed every line I ever drew for myself. It terrifies me how much power you have to hurt me now."

Paisley's hand came up to cup his cheek, her touch infinitely gentle. "I could say the same about you. But some things are worth the risk, Ben. What we have, it's worth facing Carson's anger, worth stepping into the light, worth making real."

Benedict turned his face to press a kiss into her palm. "I know. And we will. After his appointment. Once we're sure he's strong enough."

As if summoned by their conversation, Benedict's phone chimed with an incoming message. He reached for it, checking the screen.

"It's from Penn," he reported. "Confirmation that Flintly's digital presence has been erased. Blackwater is searching for their missing operative, but the trail leads nowhere."

Another message arrived moments later, this one from Carson.

"Well?" Paisley prompted, noting the change in Benedict's expression.

"Carson. He says he's feeling much better and wants us both to come for dinner next week. Says he has news to share." Benedict looked up from the screen, meeting Paisley's gaze. "Think it's about Kinsley?"

"Almost certainly," she replied with a small smile. "You've seen how they look at each other."

Benedict set the phone aside, pulling Paisley back into his arms. "Then we'll have dinner. Hear his news. And afterward, tell him ours."

She nestled against his chest, her body warm and alive against his. "One more week of secrets," she murmured, already drifting toward sleep. "Then everything changes."

"Not everything," Benedict countered softly, pressing a kiss to her forehead. "Not us. Not what matters most."

Paisley's breathing deepened as sleep claimed her, the events of the day finally taking their toll. Benedict remained awake, holding her close.

CHAPTER SIXTEEN

BENEDICT

BENEDICT ADJUSTED HIS TIE FOR THE THIRD TIME. PAISLEY finally stepped in, batting his hands away to fix it herself.

"You're acting like we're heading to our execution," she teased, smoothing the silk against his chest. "It's just dinner with Carson."

"And Kinsley," Benedict reminded her. "And afterward, we tell your brother that I've been sleeping with his sister for nearly two months. Oh, and the fact that I nearly got her killed. Twice."

Paisley's lips curved into a smile. "When you put it that way, it does sound like we're heading to an execution. Yours, specifically."

Benedict didn't return her smile. A week had passed since they'd eliminated Flintly, a week of planning exactly how to tell Carson about their relationship. With her brother's doctor appointment confirming his recovery was progressing well, they'd run out of excuses to maintain their secret.

"He's going to feel betrayed," Benedict said, his voice tight. "Especially by me. Twelve years of friendship, of trust, and I've been lying to his face for weeks."

Paisley's hands stilled on his tie, her expression softening. "We've both been lying. And yes, he'll be angry. But Carson loves us both. He'll come around."

"You can't know that."

"I've known him my entire life," Paisley countered. "He's stubborn and protective, but he's not unreasonable. And he's been happier lately. Kinsley's changed him."

Benedict nodded. Carson had indeed seemed different since Kinsley Ellis had entered his life—less rigid, more open. Perhaps that would work in their favor.

"We should go," he said, checking his watch. "Traffic will be heavy."

As they drove to Carson's apartment, Benedict replayed worst-case scenarios in his mind. Carson throwing him out. Carson ending their friendship. Carson demanding Paisley move back to her own apartment.

Paisley's hand settled on his thigh, a gentle pressure that anchored him to the present. "Stop catastrophizing," she said softly. "I can hear the gears turning from here."

Benedict covered her hand with his own, grateful for her steady presence. "Force of habit. I prepare for contingencies."

"Some things can't be prepared for," she replied. "We'll adapt, whatever happens."

The words struck him as profoundly true. For someone who had built his career on control and calculation, the past two months with Paisley had been an exercise in adaptation, to unexpected emotions, to vulnerability, to a happiness he'd never allowed himself to imagine possible.

Carson's apartment building came into view, its sleek glass facade reflecting the evening sun. Benedict parked in the underground garage, stealing a moment to pull Paisley close for a kiss before they exited the car.

"For luck," he murmured against her lips.

"We don't need luck," she replied with characteristic confidence. "We have each other."

The elevator ride to Carson's penthouse was silent, a final moment of calm before the storm. When the doors opened, Kinsley greeted them, her smile warm and welcoming.

"Perfect timing," she said, accepting the bottle of wine Benedict had brought. "Carson's just finishing up a call. Come in."

The apartment was transformed from the stark, minimalist space Benedict remembered. Kinsley had added colorful throw pillows on the sofa, fresh flowers on the dining table, and the subtle scent of her perfume lingered in the air. It reminded him of how Paisley had changed his own space.

Carson emerged from his office moments later, moving with only a slight stiffness. "Sorry about that," he said, embracing Paisley briefly before shaking Benedict's hand. "Client emergency."

"On a Saturday?" Paisley asked, arching an eyebrow.

"Some people don't understand the concept of weekends," Carson replied with a rueful smile. "But I've implemented a new policy. No work calls after seven. Kinsley's orders."

The casual way he referenced Kinsley's influence over his schedule wasn't lost on Benedict.

Dinner proceeded pleasantly enough, with conversation flowing easily between the four of them. Carson appeared relaxed, more animated than Benedict had seen him in years. Occasionally, he caught Carson watching him and Paisley with an unreadable expression, but each time, Carson would redirect his attention to another topic before Benedict could analyze it further.

As they finished the main course, Carson cleared his throat, setting down his wine glass. "Kinsley and I have some news we wanted to share with you both."

Paisley glanced at Benedict.

"Kinsley and I are officially dating," Carson announced, his hand finding hers on the table.

The room fell silent before Benedict raised an eyebrow. "That's your news?"

Carson glanced at Kinsley and then back at Benedict. "Yeah, why?"

"You took a fucking bullet for her, man. Of course you two are dating. You love her."

"Well, yeah, but—"

"That's wonderful," Paisley interrupted, kicking Benedict under the table. Her smile was genuine. "I'm so happy for you both."

Carson seemed to relax, only shooting Benedict a quick glare.

"Thank you," Kinsley said. "It's been... well, not the easiest. But... it feels right."

"It does," Carson agreed, his expression softening when he looked at her before turning back to Benedict and Paisley. His expression shifted.

The temperature in the room seemed to drop ten degrees. Kinsley glanced between them, her hand finding Carson's on the table as if to steady him.

"Carson," Paisley began, her voice carefully measured, "there's something we wanted to talk to you about tonight."

God, she was going to do it.

Fuck.

"I bet there is," Carson replied, his tone neutral but his eyes never leaving Benedict's face. "Something you've been meaning to tell me for a while now?"

Benedict's mind raced. Carson looked at him not with confusion but with something closer to disappointment.

"You know," Benedict said in a low voice. It wasn't a question.

Carson's expression didn't change. "Know what, Ben? My best friend of twelve years. Why don't you tell me exactly what it is you think I might know."

Benedict reached for Paisley's hand under the table, finding it already reaching for his.

"Carson," Kinsley said in a warning tone.

"No, darling. I think Benedict has something to say. Or maybe my sweet, honest, little sister? Anything you'd like to tell me, Paisley?"

Paisley's hand tightened around Benedict's, but he responded before she could. It would be better for him to take Carson's wrath.

"Your sister and I are together," Benedict said, meeting his friend's gaze directly. "We have been for two months. And we know we should have told you from the beginning."

"How long were you planning to wait before telling me about the two of you?" Carson's expression remained perfectly controlled. It was almost more terrifying than seeing him lose his temper, which Benedict had witnessed on more than one occasion.

"Tonight, Cars." Benedict set down his glass, buying precious seconds to compose himself. "We were going to tell you tonight, after dinner."

"How convenient," Carson replied. "And if I hadn't brought it up first?"

"He's telling the truth, we planned to tell you," Paisley insisted, recovering her composure. "That's why we're here. To be honest with you."

Carson leaned back in his chair, studying them both. "Honest. Funny, I would say that you two don't know the meaning of the word, with all your little secrets."

"You're one to talk," Benedict ground his jaw as he nodded towards Kinsley. "Don't go calling our kettle black, Mr. Pot."

"That was different."

"The fuck it was." Benedict let go of Paisley's hand before he squeezed it too tight.

"Two fucking months of lies, Benedict. Of pretending to be just friends in my presence. Of staying silent during our daily meetings. Of you, Pai, visiting me in the hospital and never once mentioning that you'd moved into his fucking penthouse."

Paisley grimaced. "How did you know?"

"I've had my suspicions for weeks," Carson replied. "The way you look at each other when you think I'm not watching. The careful distance you maintain in my presence. But I wasn't certain until after I was shot."

"After?" Paisley questioned.

"Penn let it slip that you were staying at Benedict's. When I asked why, he turned an interesting shade of white and mumbled something about your apartment building having maintenance issues." Carson's lips curved in a humorless smile. "Penn's many things, but a good liar isn't one of them."

"We didn't want to complicate your recovery," Benedict said, meeting his friend's gaze directly. "You had enough to deal with."

"How fucking considerate of you, Benny," Carson replied, the edge in his voice unmistakable now. "My best friend and my sister didn't want to 'complicate' things by being honest with me. Tell me, was that before or after you fucked her in my office during the Mental Health gala?"

Paisley gasped. "How did you—"

"Fucking security cameras, Pai. I check them randomly. Imagine my surprise when reviewing footage from that night. I very nearly bleached my eyes. On my fucking desk? Really?"

Benedict closed his eyes briefly, another oversight coming back to haunt him. Of course Carson would review security footage from major events. Of course there would be evidence of their transgression. He'd been so focused on Paisley that night that he'd neglected basic surveillance countermeasures.

God, he was an idiot.

"Carson," Kinsley intervened, her voice firm. "Maybe we should all take a breath."

"I'm perfectly calm," Carson replied, though the tension in his jaw suggested otherwise. "I'm simply wondering why my sister and my closest friend thought I couldn't handle knowing they were fucking. Was it concern for me? Or was it cowardice?"

"We aren't just having sex," Benedict argued, straightening. "I love Paisley."

"And I love him," Paisley added, her hand on Benedict's thigh. "And it wasn't like that," Paisley protested, her cheeks flushed. "We were going to tell you about us, but then everything happened with Flintly, and then you were shot, and the timing never seemed right."

Carson's expression shifted from anger to confusion. "Flintly? As in Dawson Flintly? What the fuck does Dawson Flintly have to do with this?"

Benedict and Paisley exchanged a glance, realizing they'd inadvertently opened another door they'd planned to approach more carefully.

"Flintly was targeting Crest Strategies," Benedict explained, choosing his words carefully. "Using Paisley to get to us. It became... complicated."

"Complicated how?" Carson's voice had dropped dangerously low.

"Flintly kidnapped me," Paisley said quietly. "Locked me in a shipping container during that heatwave three weeks ago. Ben saved me."

The color drained from Carson's face. "What the fuck? You were fucking kidnapped and neither of you thought to tell me?"

"You were dealing with Ashford and then you were recovering from a gunshot wound," Benedict reminded him. "And we handled it."

"Handled it," Carson repeated. "And where is Flintly now?"

Another loaded glance between Benedict and Paisley. "Gone," Benedict said simply. "He won't be a problem anymore."

Understanding dawned in Carson's eyes. "You fucking killed him."

It wasn't a question, but Benedict nodded once in confirmation.

"So let me get this straight," he said after a moment, his face turning a deep red. "You two have been in a secret relationship for two months. During that time, you've been fucking my little sister. Paisley was kidnapped by a former employee with a grudge. You rescued her, eliminated the threat, and decided not to tell me any of this."

Carson's chair crashed to the floor as he shot to his feet. "You think you can just—" His voice broke as he began pacing, hands clenching and unclenching at his sides.

Benedict rose slowly, palms out. "Cars, listen—"

Carson whirled, his face contorted. The punch came out of nowhere. His knuckles collided with Benedict's cheekbone in an explosion of white-hot pain. Benedict's head snapped sideways, vision blurring as copper flooded his mouth. His legs buckled. He stumbled backward, shoulder slamming into the wall as he fought to stay upright.

"Ben!" Paisley's scream pierced the ringing in his ears.

"Carson, stop it!" Kinsley lunged forward, grabbing Carson's arm.

Benedict steadied himself against the wall, tasting blood where his teeth had cut into his cheek. Carson shook off Kinsley's grip and advanced again, shoulders bunched, eyes wild.

"It's okay," Benedict managed, raising one hand while the other covered his throbbing face. "Let him."

"The hell it is!" Paisley moved to intercept her brother.

"Pai, don't." Benedict straightened, meeting Carson's furious gaze. "I deserve it. I know I fucked up, you and I both did. I betrayed your trust, Cars. I lied to your face for months." He lowered his hand from his face, exposing the damage. "If this is what you need, I understand. I'm sorry."

Carson's chest heaved as he stared at Benedict. Then his fist shot forward again, connecting with Benedict's jaw. Pain exploded through Benedict's skull as his head rocked back.

Before he could recover, Carson grabbed his shoulders and yanked him forward into a crushing embrace.

"You stupid bastard," Carson's voice was ragged against Benedict's ear. "You saved her. Thank you for protecting her when I couldn't."

Benedict froze, arms hanging at his sides as his brain struggled to process the shift. Slowly, he returned the embrace, relief washing through him.

The moment shattered as Carson's fist drove into his stomach. Benedict doubled over, air evacuating his lungs in a violent rush as he dropped to one knee.

"That's for fucking my sister against my fucking desk," Carson growled, standing over him. "My fucking desk, Ben. I eat lunch there."

Benedict couldn't respond, fighting to breathe through the pain radiating through his abdomen. He managed a weak nod, acknowledging the fairness of the blow.

"Are you fucking done?" Paisley demanded, kneeling beside Benedict, her hand on his back.

Carson looked down at them both, the fury draining from his face. "Yeah," he said quietly. "I'm done."

"God, you're annoying," Paisley growled at her brother.

"I concur," Kinsley muttered, eyes narrowed at Carson as she crossed her arms over her chest.

Carson turned to Kinsley. "Did you know about any of this?"

She shook her head. "Not until tonight. Notice how I didn't lose my shit."

"Yeah, well, it wasn't your desk with your best friend and your sister."

"Paisley and I are friends and I fucked her brother. She didn't lose her shit." Kinsley raised an eyebrow. "Try again."

Carson winced as he ran a bloody fist through his dark hair. "The secrecy I understand," Carson said finally. "Not that I like it, but I understand the reasoning. What I don't understand, and what hurts the most, is why you thought you needed to hide your relationship from me in the first place."

The question caught Benedict off guard. He'd expected continued anger about the deception, not this pivot to their original decision to keep their relationship secret. His face throbbed, and Kinsley brought Paisley a damp napkin from the table to clean Benedict's split lip and bloody nose.

"You told the guys and me that your sister was off limits years ago."

"Yeah, when she was a dumb horny teenager, and—"

"Hey!" Paisley whipped around and glared at Carson.

"*And*," Carson emphasized the word. "And she was making heart eyes at you every time you were around. I'm not fucking blind." He shook his head. "I just didn't want her hurt when she was at the age where kids make dumb mistakes."

Paisley returned to cleaning Benedict's skin.

"Did you think so little of me?" Carson asked, genuine hurt evident in his voice as he went to the cabinet and pulled out a first aid kit. "Did you think I couldn't handle seeing two people I care about find happiness together?"

"It wasn't that simple," Benedict said, grimacing at the pain the movement caused. "You're not just her brother, Cars. You're my oldest friend. My business partner. There are twelve years of history and trust that I betrayed by developing feelings for Paisley."

"Developing feelings?" Carson repeated with a short laugh and he shoved the kit at Paisley. "Ben, you've been in love with my sister for years."

Benedict stared at him, momentarily speechless. "You knew?"

"Of course I fucking knew. I've watched you look at her like she hung the moon since she was in college." Carson shook his head. "I figured you'd either act on it eventually or you wouldn't. That was your choice. But I never thought you'd hide it from me when you finally did."

"We should have trusted you," Benedict said to Carson. "I'm sorry we didn't."

Carson's gaze shifted between them, his expression softening. "I'm still pissed," he clarified. "But not about you two being together. I'm angry about the secrets. About being kept in the dark while my sister was in danger. About not being trusted with the truth."

"That's fair," Benedict acknowledged. "And deserved. Could've done without you rearranging my fucking face, but I understand."

Carson moved to the bar in the corner of the dining room. He poured himself a measure of scotch, his back to them as he spoke. "So what happens now?"

"That depends on you," Benedict replied honestly, pushing Paisley's hand away so he could stand too. "On whether our friendship can recover from this."

Carson turned, leaning against the bar. "Our friendship has survived worse," he said after a moment, offering Benedict a glass with scotch. Benedict took it. "But things will need to change at the office. We need clear boundaries about your relationship and how it affects Crest Strategies. Starting with you two having a lifetime ban from being anywhere near my office together. God, I had to burn that desk when I saw the video."

Benedict hid his smile by downing the scotch. It burned his split lip and his throat. "Of course."

"And no more secrets," Carson added firmly, gesturing with his own glass of scotch. "I mean it. No more of this protecting me from the truth bullshit."

Carson returned to the table, setting his glass down. "We're not done talking about this," he said, his gaze fixed on Benedict, who helped Paisley up from the floor and walked with her back to the table. Kinsley joined too. "Especially about Flintly. But it can wait until tomorrow."

The remainder of the evening passed in a strange limbo between tension and tentative reconciliation. When they finally left, Carson hugged Paisley. To Benedict, he offered a handshake and a look that clearly communicated their conversation would continue in private. Maybe with another black eye involved.

In the elevator descending to the parking garage, Paisley leaned against Benedict, exhaling slowly. "That went better than I expected."

"Speak for yourself," he muttered, wincing as he brought his thumb up and touched his swollen lip. "He's still pissed."

"Yes, but not about us being together. About the deception." She looked up at him. "He'll forgive us, Ben. It'll take time, but he will."

"I hope so. I love that man like he was my brother."

"Ew. Then you'd be my brother. Please never say that again."

"Whatever you say, sis."

She punched him in the shoulder.

EPILOGUE
PAISLEY

Two Years Later

PAISLEY SMOOTHED THE SILK OF HER DEEP BLUE bridesmaid dress as she watched her brother dance with his new wife. Carson had never looked happier, his usual rigid posture relaxed as he gazed down at Kinsley. Her white gown caught the light from the crystal chandeliers overhead, transforming her into some kind of modern queen.

The estate they'd chosen for the wedding was spectacular. Manicured gardens stretching down to the water, a massive stone mansion with floor-to-ceiling windows, and enough security to satisfy even Jenna Brigg's exacting standards. The crème de la crème of Manhattan society filled the reception hall, mingling with Kinsley's influencer friends and business connections in a strange cultural collision that somehow worked.

Paisley sipped her champagne, her gaze drifting across the room to where Penn was staring at his phone, avoiding conversation with anyone who looked at him.

James stood with the governor and several state senators, his easy charm and quick wit making them laugh at something Paisley couldn't hear. As Carson's legal expert, James had worked hard over the last year and a half to keep Crest Strategies clear of all the slander that had threatened it.

And then there was Tanner, standing in a corner with his wife of three months, Blair Winters. Their relationship had begun as a secret and professional arrangement, from what little Benedict had shared, and had erupted into something so volatile that the entire office had placed bets on how quickly it would implode. But despite their completely opposite personalities, both were still breathing.

Paisley watched as Blair tugged on Tanner's neck, making him lean down so she could whisper something in his ear that actually made Tanner smile. An honest-to-god smile that transformed his usually stony features into something almost approachable.

Miracles did happen, apparently.

Paisley's gaze finally found their final target. Benedict, positioned perfectly at the edge of the room where he could observe everything while remaining unobtrusive. Her Benedict, still monitoring things even at his best friend's wedding.

Some habits never changed.

She made her way toward him, weaving through clusters of guests. The two-carat emerald-cut diamond on her left hand caught the light as she moved. He'd proposed six weeks earlier. The spring wedding date was already set.

"You're surveilling a wedding reception," she observed as she reached his side, slipping her arm through his. "Some people would call that paranoid."

"Some people wouldn't notice the senator's security detail carrying concealed weapons, or the fact that the governor's chief of staff has been drinking water instead of champagne to stay alert." Benedict's lips curved in a smile as he looked down at her. "Old habits."

"At least you're not wearing an earpiece."

"It wouldn't match the tuxedo."

Paisley laughed, leaning into him. After eighteen months together, they'd settled into a rhythm that felt both comfortable and exciting. Their attraction certainly hadn't dimmed with time.

"Carson looks happy," Benedict observed, his gaze shifting to where her brother continued to dance with Kinsley, oblivious to everyone around them.

"He is happy," Paisley confirmed. "So am I."

Benedict's arm slipped around her waist, pulling her closer. "Even though I've been driving you crazy with wedding plans?"

"Especially because you've been driving me crazy with wedding plans. Who knew the great Benedict Astor would turn into such a perfectionist about flower arrangements and seating charts?"

"I approach all operations with appropriate thoroughness."

"You made three florists cry, Ben."

"Yeah. Yeah I did," he replied with a grin.

Paisley shook her head, fighting a smile. It was endearing, if occasionally terrifying to vendors who underestimated his attention to detail.

After both Paisley and Benedict gave their speeches, handing the microphones up to family members, the crowd settled in for the inevitable and Paisley seized her opportunity.

She leaned up, her lips brushing Benedict's ear as she whispered, "I want you to fuck me in the garden maze."

The change in his posture was immediate. His eyes darkened as he turned to her, one eyebrow arched in question.

"Now?" he asked, his voice dropping to that register that never failed to send heat through her core.

"Right now," she confirmed. "While everyone's distracted by speeches. I've been thinking about it all day; you, me, that secluded fountain at the center of the maze."

Benedict's expression shifted to one of mild exasperation. "You already found the center of the maze?"

"Of course I did. I explored while you were doing security checks this morning." Paisley tugged gently at his arm. "Come on. Live a little." She let her free hand drift down his chest, stopping just above his belt.

Benedict captured her wrist, his grip firm. "You're incorrigible and I'm apparently incapable of denying you anything."

Paisley grinned triumphantly. "Is that a yes?"

"It's a 'we have exactly twelve minutes before the speeches end and they start looking for us for the cake cutting,'" he replied, already guiding her toward the French doors that led to the gardens.

They slipped outside into the warm summer evening, the sounds of the reception fading behind them as they made their way across the terrace and down the stone steps to the garden. The moon hung full and bright overhead, illuminating the carefully trimmed hedges of the maze with silver light.

"Here's the deal," Paisley said, her heart pounding as they stood at the entrance of the maze. The cool night air doing little to temper the heat rising within her.

"Deal? What deal?"

She turned to Benedict, a playful grin tugging at her lips. "Give me a thirty-second head start. When you find me, you get to fuck me."

Benedict's eyes darkened, and he nodded. "Sounds like a fun game."

"I thought so," she shot back, already stepping into the maze. "Thirty seconds. Don't cheat."

She gathered the bottom of her dress in her hands and took off, ditching her heels at the entrance. The hedges towered over her, casting long shadows in the moonlight. She'd never been a runner, and her lungs questioned what she was doing from the first ten seconds onwards. But excitement and arousal coursed through her veins. Benedict's footsteps echoed through the maze when he entered, and she forced herself to be as quiet as she could. The giggles she had to swallow made it more difficult than it needed to be. Leaves rustled as she brushed against the hedges.

Paisley darted left. Then left again. Then a right. Her heart raced as she tried to outmaneuver him. She thought she heard him behind her, only to have his footsteps echo from a different path entirely.

She found a small alcove hidden behind a particularly thick hedge and ducked inside, pressing her back against the cool leaves. Paisley forced her lungs to relax to keep her ragged breaths quiet. For a whole few seconds, she held her breath entirely as she strained to listen for

Benedict. Silence greeted her, the only sound the distant hum of the reception and the rustle of leaves overhead. Her chest heaved as she released the breath slowly.

She'd managed to hide from him.

A cocky smile crossed over her face seconds before an arm wrapped around her waist, pulling her back against a hard chest. Benedict's voice was a low growl in her ear. "Got you."

"Shit! You scared me," she yelped, letting one of the giggles free.

Benedict's chest rose and fell just as rapidly as hers, his breath hot on her neck. "You could never hide from me."

"I feel like we should have multiple tests for that. Just to be certain." She tilted her head back, grinning up at him. He pecked her forehead and nodded.

"Okay. We'll do multiple tests. but now..." Benedict spun her around, his mouth capturing hers in a devouring kiss. Paisley's hands tangled in his hair, pulling him closer, needing more.

"Do I get my prize now?" Benedict murmured against her lips, his hands already roaming her body.

Paisley nodded, pulling up her dress to give him better access. Benedict's eyes widened. Paisley beamed up at him.

"Figured I'd save a pair from your ruthlessness," she said, dragging his hand up her leg to her bare ass. "Plus, easy access." Not that her thongs were particularly difficult to navigate around. And true to his word, he'd replaced every pair of underwear he'd torn.

A wicked grin spread across his face. "Fuck, Pai. You're perfect."

He turned her around, pushing her skirt up past her waist. His hands gripped her hips, positioning her how he wanted. Paisley braced herself, spreading her legs for a wider stance. Her breath hitched as Benedict's fingers trailed down her spine.

Benedict took her arms, pulling them behind her back and holding them with one hand. His other hand slid between her legs. She was already wet. The anticipation of him finding and fucking her in the maze had done its job marvelously. He swore, his fingers sliding through her folds, teasing her entrance.

"You're soaked," he growled, inserting two fingers into her. She gasped, her hips bucking against his hand. "You liked being chased."

Paisley nodded, her breath coming in ragged gasps as Benedict's fingers worked their magic. He curled them inside her, his palm grinding against her clit. Her body trembled, her orgasm already building.

Benedict removed his fingers, leaning over and placing them in her mouth. She licked and sucked them clean, moaning at the taste of her own arousal. The familiar sound of a clinking belt and zipper unzipping came from behind her. Then, without preamble, he slammed into her, filling her completely.

Paisley cried out, her body stretching to accommodate him. Benedict's grip on her wrists tightened, his hips pistoning against her ass as he fucked her hard and fast. The sound of their bodies slapping together filled the alcove, their ragged breaths echoing through the maze.

"I liked chasing you," Benedict groaned, "I liked letting you think you got away."

"I thought I did."

"You never will." He slammed all the way in and stopped moving. Instead, he leaned over her, grasping her by the front of the neck with his free hand. "Your fucking mine, Pai. Mine."

Paisley circled her hips, trying to get some sort of friction as he pressed into her. "Yours," she gasped with his fingers around her neck. "And you're mine. Now fuck me."

He made a satisfied sound at her words, pulling out until only the tip was inside her. She waited there, needing him balls deep again. Benedict released her wrists, his hands moving to her hips.

"As you wish."

She swore as he drove into her with a renewed passion. Bracing her hands on her thighs, she arched her back, meeting his thrusts. She couldn't think. Couldn't breathe. Could only focus on the orgasm building inside her.

"Faster," she gasped.

He honored her request, snaking one hand around to find her clit.

"Oh god, yes. F-fuck. Don't stop, Ben. Please don't stop." She was so fucking close.

His fingers circled the sensitive bud, sending shockwaves of pleasure through her. Paisley's body convulsed, her orgasm slammed into her and she nearly fell; would've if Benedict didn't notice and wrap his arm around her lower stomach. He held her while she screamed his name, her body clenching around him as she rode out the waves of pleasure.

Benedict groaned, his hips faltering, his thrusts slower as hot cum filled her. "Shit, that was good," he said, pulling her back up by the neck to kiss her cheek. "You're right. We need to do that again."

"We could try the woods some time. I read a book where they did that."

"You'll have to let me borrow it."

"Fuck yeah. Lots of fun ideas in there."

"I love it already."

Finally, Benedict pulled out, turning her around to capture her mouth in a slow, languid kiss.

Benedict broke it, his breath ragged as he rested his forehead against hers. He tucked himself back into his pants, his eyes never leaving hers. A wicked grin spread across his face. "I half considered making you walk back in there with my release dripping down your thighs."

Paisley raised an eyebrow. "Wouldn't be the first time. What's stopping you?"

Benedict paused, his fingers already working to loosen his tie. "Because I want to take care of you. Good practice for the rest of our lives." He dropped to his knees, the gravel crunching beneath him. Paisley gathered the skirt of her dress, lifting it to expose her thighs as a soft smile crossed her lips. Benedict lifted one of her legs, draping it over his shoulder.

"You steady?"

She nodded placing a hand on his head, her fingers tangling in his hair.

He wet his tie with his mouth, the silk darkening with his saliva.

Paisley watched, her heart softening in her chest as her handsome wonderful man brought his tie to her inner thigh. He cleaned her gently, the cool silk soft against her skin. She shivered, her grip on his hair tightening.

"I love you, Benny," she murmured, her voice barely above a whisper. Benedict glanced up at her, his ice-blue gaze meeting hers. He pressed a soft kiss to her inner thigh.

"I love you too, Pai."

Paisley eased up on his hair, running her fingers through it. He'd let it grow out longer than she'd seen it in years. She liked it.

Benedict continued to clean her, his tie darkening. When he was finished, he pressed one last kiss just above her center before lowering her leg. He stood, his eyes never leaving hers as he tucked his tie back into his pocket. Paisley let her dress fall, smoothing it down with her hands. She reached up, cupping his cheek. "Thank you," she said.

Benedict turned his head, pressing a kiss to her palm. "Anything and everything for you," he replied. He wrapped his arms around her, pulling her close and Paisley rested her head against his chest, listening to the steady beat of his heart.

Music drifted from the reception, a new song starting. The muffled notes of a slow song drifted through the hedges. Benedict's hand slid to the small of her back.

"They'll notice we're missing," he murmured against her hair.

"Well, they noticed the entire time we were sneaking around before," she replied, swaying to the distant melody. "I don't care if they notice now."

Benedict chuckled, the sound vibrating through his chest. "Carson's already threatened to kill me once today."

"My brother needs to mind his own business." Paisley pulled back just enough to look up at him, smoothing her thumb over his cheek. "Dance with me."

A rare, genuine smile crossed Benedict's face as he guided her into a proper dance position, one hand at her waist, the other taking her hand. They swayed and turned together, in sync despite the limited space.

"Never thought I'd dance with you in a hedge maze," he said, spinning her.

Paisley followed his lead, grinning. "Never thought you'd do a lot of things with me in a hedge maze."

His chuckle warmed her in the cool night air. Benedict pulled her closer, their dance becoming less structured and more an excuse to hold each other.

"Twelve years of wanting. Watching. Waiting for you to fall in love with someone else," he murmured against her temple.

"And two years of having. Doing life. Loving you more than I've loved anyone else." Paisley tilted her chin up as she rested her head on his chest.

"And a lifetime ahead to find something new to love every single day."

"I wouldn't have done it any other way."

READ THE FIRST CHAPTER IN THE NEXT NOVELLA IN THE BILLIONAIRES OF CREST STRATEGIES SERIES

A DARK BILLIONAIRE ROMANCE NOVELLA

SALVAGED
Vows

ELORA RAE

CHAPTER 1

BLAIR

BLAIR WINTERS WAS SO SICK OF MEN IN SUITS TELLING HER she was wrong.

"Ms. Winters, we—"

"It's doctor. Dr. Winters," she corrected, seething inside.

"Dr. Winters, we simply cannot allow testing to continue after these allegations." The FDA representative's voice droned like a lazy insect.

Blair bit her tongue until she tasted copper. Three doctorates, seventeen patents, and a breakthrough that could help thousands of paralyzed patients, yet these bureaucrats looked at her like she was a hysterical girl playing with dangerous toys. She'd spent her entire career proving herself in labs dominated by men who assumed her success was luck or affirmative action or sleeping with the right professor. Never again.

"The whistleblower report raises serious concerns about potential weapons applications."

Blair squared her shoulders, staring down the panel of five men and one woman who held her life's work in their bureaucratic hands. The conference room felt too small, too warm, with walls that seemed to inch closer with each passing minute.

"The allegations are completely false," she said, fighting to keep her voice steady. "My research has never, not once, been directed toward offensive applications. The neural regeneration properties of VX-7 have documented therapeutic potential for spinal injuries."

The woman, Dr. Clyborne from the NIH, glanced down at the report in front of her. "The molecular structure bears striking similarities to VX nerve agents. You understand our concern."

"Similar is not the same. Water bears a striking similarity to hydrogen peroxide, but one hydrates you and the other kills you." Blair took a breath, reining herself in. "The whistleblower deliberately misconstrued early test results."

"Nevertheless," said the man at the center, a representative for the Department of Defense. "All testing must cease pending investigation. Your lab will be sealed effective immediately."

Five years of research. Millions in funding. All her test subjects who were finally showing promising nerve regeneration. Gone because someone had lied.

"You can't—" Blair started.

"We can, and we have." Andrews shuffled his papers. "This meeting is adjourned."

Blair remained seated as they filed out, her mind racing through options that dwindled with each passing second. By tomorrow, this would hit the news. Brilliant Scientist Develops Illegal Bioweapon. Her reputation would be shredded before she could defend herself.

Her phone vibrated. A news alert: Breaking: Winters Biomedical Under Investigation for Illegal Weapons Development.

Shit. It had already begun.

———

THREE HOURS LATER, BLAIR STOOD IN HER EMPTIED LAB, security tape crossing the entrance like yellow crime scene markers. Two uniformed guards watched as she collected personal items from her desk. She'd been given fifteen minutes. Fifteen minutes to salvage something from half a decade of work.

"Dr. Winters?" Her research assistant, Constantine, hovered in the doorway. "I'm so sorry about this."

Blair tried to smile but couldn't quite manage it. "Not your fault."

"I know you weren't developing weapons," he said, voice low. "We all know."

She nodded, throat tight. "Tell the others... tell them I'll fix this."

As she left the building, carrying a pathetic box of framed degrees and family photos, Blair's phone rang. Unknown number.

"Hello?"

"Dr. Winters." A crisp male voice. "My name is Carson Crest, CEO of Crest Strategies. I believe we can help with your situation."

Blair nearly laughed. "Unless you can convince the Department of Defense I'm not developing bioweapons, I seriously doubt it."

"Actually, that's exactly what we do."

"You're a PR firm." Blair walked faster toward her car, scanning the growing crowd of reporters near the parking garage.

"We're a reputation management company with specialized experience in crisis situations like yours."

Blair reached her car and dumped her box in the passenger seat before sliding behind the wheel. "My crisis isn't a sex scandal or some celebrity drama where someone said something stupid. My entire life's work has been misrepresented as biological terrorism. I think there's a bit of a difference there."

"Which is why I would like to meet you personally."

Resting her head against the wheel, Blair sighed.

"I don't see the point. The investigation on my life's work has already begun and just like with placebo experiments, they're going to see what they want to see and ruin me further." She snorted, sitting up and slumping with her head against the headrest. "Besides, with my work frozen, I won't be able to pay for your help."

"I'm sure we can work something out, Ms. Winters. That is," he paused, "if you actually want to fix this."

"Of course I want to fix this!" Blair snapped, slamming the palm of her hand against the steering wheel. "What they are doing is shitty and based on a lie. Do you know how many people with paralysis I could help if these idiots would just let me work?"

The billionaire, whose company had saved celebrities, politicians, and corporations from complete destruction, remained silent.

Taking a deep breath to calm herself again, Blair shifted her grip on her phone. "When can we meet?" she asked.

"How quickly can you get to Manhattan?"

Blair glanced at the reporters now recording her sitting in her car. Her phone was already flooded with notifications: colleagues distancing themselves, conference invitations rescinded, and most alarmingly, a message from her primary funding source initiating termination procedures.

"I can be there in two hours."

Blair immediately began talking to herself as soon as the call ended. It had driven her ex-husband crazy when she did that, but at least it kept her sane.

"Complete idiots. Molecular similarity? By that logic, we should ban table salt because chlorine is toxic. Should I have simplified it more? Used smaller words? Drawn them a picture? God, I need to call Dr. Kustka at Cornell. He'll vouch for the therapeutic applications. And the trial patients. What happens to them now? Did the panel care about how many fucking lives this is helping? No. God, funding will freeze by morning. Five years of work. My entire reputation. Think, Blair, think..."

She realized she'd been talking out loud for several minutes, her words tumbling faster as her mind raced through collapsing possibilities. With a deep breath, she started the car and pulled out of the parking lot, ignoring the reporters tapping on her windows.

———

THE CREST STRATEGIES BUILDING TOWERED OVER THE street below, gleaming with all of its glass and steel edges. Blair stepped from her car feeling decidedly underdressed in the black pants and emerald blouse she'd hastily changed into at a rest stop bathroom.

At the reception desk, a sleek blonde woman smiled. "Dr. Winters. Welcome to Crest Strategies. Mr. Crest is expecting you."

The elevator ride to the top floor gave Blair just enough time to doubt every decision that had led her here. She'd driven straight from her lab in Connecticut without a plan beyond this meeting. If Crest Strategies couldn't help her, what then?

The doors opened to reveal a minimalist reception area where a striking woman with auburn hair pulled into a severe braid waited.

"Dr. Winters. Jenna Briggs, head of security." She extended her hand. "Thank you for coming."

Blair shook her hand, noting the woman's firm grip and the subtle bulge of a concealed weapon beneath her tailored jacket. The woman was somewhat terrifying.

"The team is assembled in the conference room," Jenna said, leading the way down a corridor.

"Team?"

"Mr. Crest has called the other head members of Crest Strategies in response to your case. Time is critical in situations like yours."

Before Blair could ask more questions, Jenna opened a door to a large conference room where four men sat around a polished table.

"Dr. Winters," said the man at the head of the table, rising. "Carson Crest. Thank you for coming. My team: Benedict Astor, operations and surveillance director," he indicated a slender man with ice-blue eyes, "and Penn Lavigne, our digital specialist." The younger man with disheveled light brown hair barely looked up from multiple screens, one of which seemed to be running facial recognition software on what looked like social media photos.

"And Tanner Whitney," Carson finished, nodding toward the fourth man.

Blair's attention shifted to the large man who was already watching her. Unlike the others in their perfect suits, Tanner Whitney simply wore a dress shirt and a tie, the sleeves rolled up to reveal full-sleeve tattoos on both forearms. Broader shoulders stretched his shirt, and for a moment, Blair wondered how much of the rest of him was tattooed. His military-short hair and the scar that bisected his left eyebrow made him look far meaner than the rest of the men present. The rotten scowl on his face didn't help either.

"Mr. Whitney handles our more... specialized security concerns," Carson explained.

Tanner's gaze swept over Blair, as though cataloging threats rather than meeting a potential client. His silence felt deliberate rather than awkward.

"We're usually a team of five, but our fifth is currently representing us in a court case. James Rothschild is our law specialist and a particularly cunning lawyer. Please, sit," Carson gestured to a chair. "We've reviewed the initial reports about your situation. Quite the mess."

Blair sank into the offered chair. "That's one word for it."

"Would you mind filling us in on what it is you've been working on?" The man Carson had referred to as Benedict asked with a reassuring nod. "It will help us determine the best way to help you."

"Right, yes. Of course," Blair tore her focus from Tanner, who was still staring at her like she'd run over his dog with her car. It was far more pleasant to look at the other three men, which was what she did. "My VX-7 compound targets damaged myelin sheaths in the central nervous system," Blair explained, unable to keep the passion from her voice. "Initial trials showed 78% neural regeneration in subjects with complete C4 spinal severance. Yes, the molecular backbone shares structural elements with organophosphates, but we've modified the binding sites to target only damaged nerve tissue. Whoever this fucking whistleblower is, they deliberately omitted the protein markers that prevent systemic toxicity."

Across the table, Tanner raised an eyebrow. However, he remained silent.

The obvious tech genius, Penn, nodded before his fingers flew across his keyboard. "The whistleblower report hit six news outlets simultaneously at 9:47 this morning. Coordinated attack."

"Which suggests this wasn't a concerned employee," Benedict added. "Likely a planned takedown."

Blair's stomach turned. She bit her lip. "You think someone

targeted me specifically? That's a large assumption to make without more data to support it."

"Your research has significant potential market value," Carson explained. "We've seen this sort of thing before. When someone develops something monumental, other people want credit and fame for it. Your pharmaceutical applications are likely worth billions, and defense applications worth more. Someone likely wants to control it."

"But why not just offer to buy me out? Why destroy me?"

"It's cheaper," Tanner finally spoke.

"Exactly. It would be cheaper to acquire distressed assets. Discredit you, devalue your company, and then acquire the research for pennies," Carson said, nodding.

Blair dropped her attention to the table, frowning as she considered their words. It made sense. In fact, it was quite smart, even if it was ruining her life.

"Mr. Whitney has experience with similar tactics in military operations," Carson explained. "His assessment is typically accurate."

Penn swiveled his chair. "I've been analyzing chatter around your company. Three venture capital firms have shown sudden interest in your patents since the allegations broke." His gaze flicked briefly to a secondary screen showing what appeared to be surveillance footage before returning to his work.

"So what do I do?" Blair asked, unable to hide the desperation edging her voice as she rubbed the hem of her sleeve between two fingers. "I deal with chemistry and pharmaceuticals. Biology, not... this." She gestured towards Penn's laptops.

"That's why I reached out to you." Carson leaned forward. "We can mount a comprehensive defense. Media strategy, legal counter-offensive, and most importantly, security protocols to protect you and your research."

"I can't afford—"

"We can discuss payment options later," Carson waved away her concern. "First, we need to understand exactly what we're dealing with. I need complete transparency from you."

Blair hesitated. Her research was her life. Sharing it meant vulnerability she wasn't comfortable with.

"We can't help if you hold back," Carson added.

"It's not that simple. My work contains proprietary elements that—"

"Are potentially being stolen as we speak," Tanner interrupted, his gaze locked on hers. "Every minute you waste increases the risk."

"But it's my life's work. I can't just—"

"It won't be yours for much longer." Tanner scoffed, lifting an eyebrow.

"Are you threatening me?"

"Of course not. Mr. Whitney has a direct approach," Benedict said, his voice diplomatic, "but unfortunately he's right. Full disclosure is your best protection."

Blair glanced from Benedict, whose reassuring smile was the absolute antithesis of the glare on Tanner's face. Who'd pissed in his coffee? Still though, he was probably right, not that she'd ever admit it. She couldn't deal with the whistleblower's fallout alone.

"Fine. Full disclosure." She pulled a small drive out of her bag. "This contains everything. My research, test results, molecular structures, everything. I want an NDA contract signed by anyone who has access to this."

"Done," Carson said with a nod. "I'll put James on it when he gets back to the office later today.

"I want a temporary one now, though, before I give it over."

Benedict was already writing something on a tablet, and he passed it to Carson first. "It's rudimentary, but it would hold up in court. Gentlemen, Ms. Winters, please sign."

They passed the tablet around the room, and Blair watched each man scrawl a signature. She rubbed the drive between her fingers as the tablet got closer to her. On second thought, maybe this was a mistake. She hesitated when the tablet got to her.

"Dr. Winters?" Carson asked from his seat. "Something wrong?"

"No, I just…"

"Sign the damn tablet," Tanner muttered under his breath, earning a glare from both Carson and Benedict.

"You wouldn't be so quick to sign if it were the most important thing in your life," she shot back, adding her glare to the mix.

Tanner merely grunted, rolling his eyes and crossing his large arms over his chest. He sank back in his chair, his attention still heavy on her.

When she finally managed to sign her signature after reading the few quick sentences Benedict had written, it felt as though her stomach was a churning whirlpool. Why did she feel like she was going to be sick?

"Here," she muttered, holding out the drive.

Penn reached for it, but Tanner intercepted it with surprising speed for a man his size. His fingers brushed Blair's in the process, and she yanked her hand back.

"I'll handle security protocols for this data," he said, his voice lower than before.

Blair fought the urge to rub her fingers where his had touched. What the hell was that?

"I need your word this stays protected," she managed, hoping her voice sounded steadier than it felt.

"Mr. Whitney's security measures are... comprehensive," Carson assured her. "Now, we should discuss immediate protective measures for you personally."

Benedict nodded. "The whistleblower report includes your home address. Not safe to return there."

She hadn't even noticed, too concerned about what it meant for her research.

Fear, which Blair had been holding at bay with anger and pure determination, finally broke through. "You think I'm in physical danger?"

Before Carson could answer, Tanner spoke again, his voice flat and certain. "Yes."

"Oh," she murmured, rubbing the end of her sleeve again. "I...I guess I could find somewhere else to stay for a while. Maybe a hotel."

This wasn't just about her research or reputation. Someone wanted what she had badly enough to destroy her for it.

"It'll be safer if we take you to a secure location. I'll have Ms. Briggs, our head of security, look into it immediately," Carson said.

"What exactly does this all mean?" she asked.

Carson glanced at Tanner, a silent communication passing between them. Tanner gave an almost imperceptible nod.

"Since this is a high-profile case, Tanner will be personally responsible for your security," Carson said. "24/7 protection until this situation is resolved."

Blair's gaze darted to Tanner, who watched her with the same unreadable expression. The thought of this intense, silent man shadowing her every move made something flutter uncomfortably in her stomach. It'd be like having the world's most imposing shadow following her around.

"I talk a lot," she blurted out. "Like, constantly. Everyone says so. I process verbally. It's how I think."

If she expected this warning to deter him, Tanner's response disappointed. He simply nodded once. "Noted."

"We need your decision, Dr. Winters," Carson pressed. "Are you engaging our services?"

Blair looked at Tanner again. His eyes held no warmth, no reassurance.

But what else was she supposed to do?

"Yes. I suppose I don't have any other choice."

"Excellent," Carson said, signaling the end of the meeting. "Once Ms. Briggs has determined a safe location, Tanner will escort you there and brief you on protocols."

As everyone rose, Blair battled against rising panic. In the span of twenty-four hours, she'd lost her lab, her reputation, and now, apparently, her freedom of movement. Everything was spiraling beyond her control, like a chemical reaction.

Tanner stepped beside her, and she had to tilt her head back to look up at him. Damn, he was even more imposing standing. "You can wait in the main lobby until I come to get you." He left without another word.

"Great," she muttered under her breath. "Just fucking great."

READ THE REST OF TANNER AND BLAIR'S STORY IN THE NEXT BILLIONAIRES OF CREST STRATEGIES NOVELLA:

SALVAGED
Vows

MAKE SURE TO CHECK OUT
ALL FIVE BOOKS IN THE
BILLIONAIRES OF CREST STRATEGIES SERIES

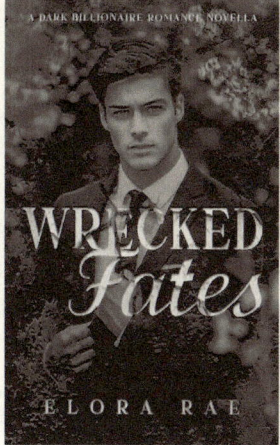

ACKNOWLEDGMENTS

I actually published *another* book. If you're reading this, it means *Tattered Secrets* is out in the world, proving once again that I have a thing for men with boundary issues and surveillance-grade devotion. This is Book Two. I should be more composed about it. I'm not.

First, thank you to my parents, who still don't quite understand why I'm writing about obsessive billionaires with questionable ethics but haven't staged an intervention yet. And to my brother, who once again did not read this book (wise), but told his friends, "Yeah, my sister's writing a whole series now," like I was someone worth bragging about. I have the best brother.

To my beta readers: thank you for strapping back in for round two. Dani R., Mariah S., Rachel H., and to Zoe M., welcome to the unhinged club. You're one of us now.

Publishing *Ruined Lies* was terrifying. Publishing this one? Slightly less terrifying, but only because I know you're here for the dark, messy, obsessive love stories too. You make it easier to be brave.

Thank you for reading, screaming, and texting your friends about morally gray men who should definitely be in therapy.

Stay obsessed,
Elora Rae

*P.S. A rating and review are like sending Benedict a love note, and you know he collects those. Just saying…

ABOUT THE AUTHOR

Elora Rae is a longtime lover of dark romance, drawn to stories about morally grey men, obsessive love, and twisted secrets. When she's not writing, Elora is probably re-reading her favorite villain origin love stories or plotting the next emotionally delicious downfall. *Ruined Lies* and *Tattered Secrets* are just the beginning.

www.ingramcontent.com/pod-product-compliance
Lightning Source LLC
Chambersburg PA
CBHW021147130626
46554CB00005B/1697